Hey There

(You with the Gun in Your Hand)

Also by Robert J. Randisi

Hey There

(You with the Gun in Your Hand)

ROBERT J. RANDISI

Thomas Dunne Books
St. Martin's Minotaur New York

THOMAS DUNNE BOOKS.
An imprint of St. Martin's Press.

HEY THERE (YOU WITH THE GUN IN YOUR HAND). Copyright © 2008 by Robert J. Randisi. All rights reserved. Printed in the United States of America. For information, address St. Martin's Press, 175 Fifth Avenue, New York, N. Y. 10010.

www.thomasdunnebooks.com
www.minotaurbooks.com

Library of Congress Cataloging-in-Publication Data

Randisi, Robert J.
   Hey there (you with the gun in your hand) : a Rat Pack mystery / Robert J. Randisi.— 1st ed.
      p. cm
   ISBN-13: 978-0-312-37642-0
   ISBN-10: 0-312-37642-1
   1. Rat Pack (Entertainers)—Fiction. 2. Casinos—Fiction. 3. Las Vegas (Nev.)—Fiction. I. Title.
   PS3568.A53H49 2008
   813'.54—dc22
                                                            2008030119

First Edition: December 2008

10 9 8 7 6 5 4 3 2 1

To Marthayn,
Hey There . . .
well, you know the rest.

Hey There

(You with the Gun in Your Hand)

Prologue

Las Vegas, Nevada
February 10, 2002

DEAN STARED OUT at the crowd from the stage and asked, "How did all these people get in my room?"

Frank said, "Keep smilin', Sam, so they can see you."

Joey said to Frank and Dean, "Stop singin' and tell the people all the good work the Mafia's doin'."

They moved around the stage like a well-oiled machine. The lines were old, but the crowd loved each and every one of them.

"Hurry up, Sam," Frank said, "the watermelon's gettin' warm."

Frank was the Leader, but Joey was the director. Not many people knew at the time that Joey wrote a lot of the jokes the Rat Packers did on stage.

Like Dean and Sammy saying in tandem, "If all the women in Texas were as ugly as yo' momma, the Lone Ranger gon' be alone for a loooong time."

Or Dean picking Sammy up in his arms and saying, "I'd like to thank the NAACP for this award."

Later I found out that the line was supposed to be, "I'd like to thank the B'nai B'rith . . ." but Dean couldn't remember the line, so he kept saying "NAACP" and they finally left it in.

And my favorite was when Sammy put his arm around Dean, and Dino said, "I'll sing with ya, I'll dance with ya, I'll pick cotton with ya, I'll even go to a Bar Mitzvah with ya, but don't touch me."

A modern crowd might have taken offense at this and many of the other lines, but the first time they were performed it wasn't to a modern crowd. It was 1960.

That was then, and this was now . . .

Okay, so it wasn't the real Rat Pack up there on stage. All of them but Joey—about my age now, eighty-three or -four—were gone. Frank was the last one to go in '98. I had attended all their funerals, because over the years they became my buddies.

This particular tribute show was at the Greek Isles Casino. Buddy Hackett's son, Sandy—Buddy went in '03, damn it—was the driving force behind it and also played Joey Bishop. He had been smart enough to get his father to record an opening. Buddy played God and did a small monologue, which was meant to set up the show.

For a while in '60 and '61 I kinda thought the guys might've just been using me to get themselves out of jams because they knew I had the town wired. But later, when I started getting invitations to shows and events, even Christmas cards, I decided we were friends—especially Dino and Frank.

Peter Lawford and I never got along, but then he fell out with Frank, too.

But Joey and me, we got along from the get-go. I had a lot of respect for Joey because he wrote a lot of the material the Rat Pack did on stage, and he wasn't bothered by the fact that Frank, Dino and Sammy got most of the accolades. Joey Bishop knew he was brilliant, and didn't need anybody else's opinion to prove it. Not for nothing did Frank call him "the Hub of the Big Wheel," giving him credit for writing most of their shtick.

It took a little longer for me and Sammy to get to know each other. The first two times I had to help the guys—during the filming of *Ocean's 11* and then at the Vegas premier of the movie six months later—I dealt mostly with Dino and Frank. But the third time, that was all Sammy's mess. . . .

✳   ✳   ✳

The show was still a few minutes from starting when Sandy Hackett came over to my front row seat.

"You comfortable, Eddie?" he asked, shaking my hand. "I'm sorry I couldn't greet you at the door. I just wanted to make sure they got you to your seat."

"I'm fine, Sandy, just fine," I said.

"Can you see okay?"

"I'm old, Sandy," I said, "but I'm not blind . . . yet."

Sandy laughed.

"I want you to tell me what you think when it's over, Eddie," he said, "and I want you to be honest. It's important to me what Eddie G thinks. After all, you were buds with them. All of them."

"You knew them, too, Sandy."

"I knew 'em through my dad," he said, "and I didn't know 'em back then, like you did. I mean, I wasn't there at the Sands, Eddie. You were."

"I know I was, Sandy," I said.

"Well, I gotta get backstage," he said. "Enjoy the show, Eddie."

He shook hands with me again.

"I'm sure I will," I said. "You're a good kid, Sandy." I looked down at the program. "Puttin' your dad in the show was brilliant."

"Wait 'til you hear him as God, Eddie. It's only at the beginning of the show, but you'll bust a gut. God speaking with Buddy Hackett's accent talking to the guys, who are supposedly up in Heaven with him, telling them about this show that was being done on earth in their honor. It's great, great."

"I'm lookin' forward to it."

It had been a long time since I'd busted a gut—in a good way. Those times are few and far between, when I've got diabetes and high blood pressure. When I either have shooting pains in or can't feel my feet. When I can't eat what I want to eat.

No wonder I spend so much time remembering the past.

One

"Between us we knew everybody in show business."

—Sammy Davis Jr.

B UDDY HACKETT WAS A RIOT.

When Joey Bishop asked me if I wanted to go and see Buddy at the Riv I jumped at the chance. Joey—a pretty funny guy himself—told me he thought Buddy Hackett was the funniest man he'd ever seen. I agreed, and since Joey had two tickets I happily went along.

Buddy was hilarious, as usual, and after he was done the three of us went to dinner at the Sahara in their Congo Room. We sat in the "Sinatra Booth," which Frank occupied whenever he was in town.

Joey was in town taking a break. He chose Vegas because Dean would be appearing at the Sands at the end of the week.

"Frank's at his house at the Cal Neva in Tahoe," Joey told me, when I asked about the other guys, "and Sammy's starting a gig in Tahoe at Harrah's."

I knew Frank had been in Washington with the Kennedys for the inaugural balls in January, but he had apparently been staying at home since then.

With Joey and Buddy in the same room I spent most of the night in stitches. They kept swapping stories—good ones, bad ones, but all funny ones. Then they started talking about the future.

"I'm talkin' to Danny Thomas about guesting on his show in the spring," Joey said. "Might be a chance for me to do my own show for his production company."

"Like he did for Andy Griffith?" Buddy said. "Dat's great, Joey."

"I liked the old name of his show," I said, "*Make Room for Daddy*. Before he switched networks and changed it to *The Danny Thomas Show*."

"If I get my own show," Joe said, "I'm just gonna call it *The Joey Bishop Show*."

"I don't blame ya," Buddy said. "I'd do the same but what would I do with a program called *The Joey Bishop Show*?"

That cracked us all up, and then Buddy started telling us some new bits he was thinking of putting in his act.

"Tell me what ya think. I walk out on stage naked." He looked at both of us eagerly.

"Totally naked?" Joey asked.

"Completely butt naked," Buddy said, "and I just stare at the audience, like this."

He screwed his face up as only Buddy could and I couldn't help myself. I started laughing.

"See?" Buddy said. "It'll work."

"Better you than me," Joey said. "I mean, I've been on stage and felt naked, but to really be naked?"

"Socks," I said.

"Huh?" Buddy looked at me.

"Shoes and socks," I said. "If you came out naked, but wearing . . . black shoes and socks, I think that'd be funnier."

Buddy thought it over, looked at Joey, and then the two of them started laughing, Buddy slapping me on the back.

By the time Joey and I left Buddy and headed back to the Sands, my sides were aching.

"How about a nightcap?" Joey asked.

Joey rarely drank, so I agreed and we went into the Silver Queen Lounge. It was late, the last set had been played by the lounge act, and we were able to sit at the bar and talk quietly.

"Still no free drinks?" Joey asked, when I paid the bartender for my bourbon and his coffee.

"Jack doesn't want to start a trend."

Joey nodded and sipped his coffee.

"What's on your mind, Joey?" I asked.

"Why does somethin' have to be on my mind?"

"Look," I said, "I had a great time tonight. Buddy's great and the two of you together are a riot. But when's the last time you invited me for a night on the town?"

"You're a smart man, Eddie," Joey said. He pointed his finger at me. "I said that first, and the rest of the guys found it out later."

"Not Peter."

"Peter's okay," Joey said, but didn't go any further.

"Where is he, Joey?" I asked. "Where's Frank?"

"He's at the Cal Neva, in Tahoe," Joey said. "He'd like you to come there."

"Why didn't he just call me?"

Joey shrugged helplessly.

"Maybe you could ask 'im when you see 'im."

"And when is that?"

"Well, hopefully tomorrow," Joey said.

"He wants me to drive to Tahoe tomorrow?"

"Fly," Joey said. "He said you can use his copter."

"Copter?"

"One of the improvements Frank made at the Cal Neva was putting in a helipad."

"Really?"

"You ever been up in a helicopter?"

"No."

"You'll love it."

"I thought the Cal Neva was only open from June through September. After all, it's a lodge, not a real hotel."

"Frank's convinced it could be a moneymaker all year round,"
Joey said. "That's why he's there, in his cabin. The casino isn't open
yet, but it will be."

"I have a job, Joey."

"I have a feeling Jack will let you go, don't you?" he asked.

No, it wasn't a feeling. I *knew* Jack Entratter, my boss, would let
me go. He'd do anything to keep Frank Sinatra happy.

"Okay, Joey," I said. "You callin' Frank tonight?"

"As soon as I get back to my room."

"Tell him I'll be there."

"Thanks, Eddie." Joey slid off his stool. "You finish your drink.
I'm gonna turn in."

"I'll have to talk to Jack first thing," I said. "Tell Frank to have
his helicopter ready by ten."

"I'll tell 'im," Joey said. " 'Night, Eddie."

"Thanks for the show and dinner, Joey."

"Sure, anytime."

The bartender came over. I could tell he was impressed. "Still hobnobbin' with the stars, huh, Eddie?"

I finished my drink and set the empty glass down on the bar.

"You got it wrong, Harry," I told him. "They're hobnobbin' with
me."

Two

FRANK ANSWERED THE DOOR HIMSELF, holding a paperback novel in one hand.

"Eddie G! How the hell are ya, pally?" He grabbed my hand and pumped it, then pulled me in, slamming the door. I looked around the cabin. His majordomo, George, was nowhere to be seen.

"Flyin' solo this time," he said, reading my mind. "Come on, come on, sit down. I'll get you a drink. Bourbon?"

"Bourbon's good, Frank."

He put the book down on the coffee table and went to the bar. There was a girl in a black dress against a yellow background on the cover. The title was *Miami Mayhem* by Anthony Rome. I picked it up and was still reading the back when he returned with the drinks.

"That came out last year," he said, handing me the glass. "I'm thinking of makin' a movie out of it. I'd play the lead, Tony Rome, a Miami private eye. There's another one, too, came out last month. It's called *The Lady in Cement*."

"Sounds interesting," I said. "Any parts for the other guys?"

"Naw," Frank said, sitting in an armchair across from me. "Well, maybe Nick Conte. I just need somebody to play the cop. Nick looks like a cop."

"Wait a minute," I said. " 'Tony Rome' is the P.I.? And the author is Anthony Rome?"

"It's a pen name," Frank said. "The guy's real name is Marvin Albert. I've talked to him once, already." He leaned forward, picked the book up, looked at it, put it down and said, "It's gonna be good. Kinda like *The Maltese Falcon* my buddy Bogey made, only in this one the guy's *ex*-partner is killed, and there's no Falcon, just a pin, a piece of jewelry. It's gonna be good," he said, again.

"I'm sure it will be." I was wondering if he was trying to convince me, or himself. I sat back and sipped my drink.

"How do you like the cabin?"

"It's great. Kind of like a rustic suite."

"Exactly," Frank said. "It's got a huge bedroom. Three, four and five never get rented out."

"Never?"

"Five is mine," Frank explained, spreading his arms. "Three is for broads—like when Marilyn comes out. She's in Reno now, making *The Misfits* with Clark Gable. I asked her to come out here, but they're givin' her a hard time about bein' late to the set."

I nodded. I'd read about that in the papers.

"And four is for guys. If you stay here, Eddie, you get four."

"That's what I'm here to talk about, isn't it, Frank?" I asked.

Not only had his copter flown me from Vegas, but his driver had brought me to cabin five from the heliport in Frank's car. Now it was just him and me, no Rat Packers, no hangers on.

"You're right, Eddie," Frank said, "and I didn't thank you for comin'. I guess Jack had to give you some time off, huh?"

"When Jack heard you wanted to see me, he gave me all the time I'd need," I said. "So now all I have to find out is, how much time *will* I need?"

"I don't know, Eddie," he said. "Maybe I should just tell you what the problem is, and then we can figure it out."

"I'm all ears, Frank."

The Chairman of the Board sat back in his chair and said, "It's Sammy, this time."

"Joey said he was playin' Harrah's, up here."

"He is," Frank said. "I offered him a cabin, but it seems like Harrah's is lettin' him stay on the premises."

"Things are startin' to change," I said.

"Not on their own, they're not," Frank said. "You know I made Jack Entratter let Sammy stay in the hotel when we play the Sands."

"I heard that."

"Well, Sammy told them at Harrah's he wasn't gonna play their place if they didn't let him have a room. So they did."

"Good for him," I said. "Now tell me he got some threatening letters, or phone calls, and I won't be surprised."

Frank laughed.

"Naw, Smokey's used to that," he said. "That wouldn't bother him at all. Ya know, he's a little guy but I don't know if the biggest part of him is his talent, or his balls."

"So if he's not gettin' threats what *is* the problem?"

"I think you oughtta go and talk to him about it, Eddie," Frank said.

"Did you tell Sammy you asked me to come?"

"I did," he said.

"And what'd he say?"

"It doesn't matter what he said," Frank answered. "Last year if you'd asked Dean if he needed help he woulda said no. Hell, if you'd asked me back in August if I needed your help to find that dame I probably woulda said no, but you did it both times. You helped Dean and you helped me. Now I'd like you to help Sam."

"Well, Frank, I'll help if he'll let me," I said.

"I'll have my driver take you over to Harrah's," Frank said, as we both stood up. "Cabin four's yours for as long as you want it."

"I didn't bring an overnight bag."

"Well, the copter can take you back to Vegas if you want, or we can buy you something to wear."

He slapped me on the back and kept his hand there while we walked to the door.

"You know, Frank, if Sammy's having trouble here in Tahoe maybe you should get somebody local—"

"We trust you, Eddie," he said, cutting me off. "I could get some local guy, but I wouldn't know him. Or I could bring some fixer out from L.A. But I trust you. We all do. You're our guy, Eddie. And your Vegas contacts? I'll bet they've got tentacles that spread all over the country, so I'm not too worried about you findin' your way around Tahoe. But talk to Sammy before you make any plans."

"Okay, Frank."

He opened the door and stepped out behind me so that we were both standing on the wooden deck. His driver was leaning against the side of the car.

"Henry," he called down, "take Eddie anywhere he wants to go."

"Yes sir, Mr. Sinatra."

I turned and shook hands with Frank.

"When you're done with Sammy either come back here or head on back to Vegas," Frank said. "Your choice. Just give me a call and let me know, huh?"

"I will, Frank."

The driver held the back door open for me, then trotted around and got behind the wheel.

"Where to, sir?" he asked.

"Harrah's, James."

"It's Henry, sir."

"And it's still Harrah's, Henry."

"Yes, sir."

Three

HARRAH'S WAS FIRST OPENED in South Lake Tahoe in Stateline, Nevada, by William F. Harrah in 1955. In '59 it moved across the street and became Harrah's Stateline Club.

The South Shore Room, where Sammy was playing, opened in '59. The 750 seat room cost $3.5 million dollars. The opening act was Red Skelton.

Since Sammy was expecting me, and Frank had given me his room number, I walked through the lobby, went right upstairs and knocked on his door. Harrah's could not have been called an integrated property by any means at that time, but this was Sammy's first appearance in Harrah's Shore Room. They obviously wanted to keep him happy, so they gave him a room in the hotel rather than making him stay off premises.

Like Frank, Sammy opened the door to his own room. Unlike Frank, Sammy was wearing a pair of six-guns in twin holsters.

"Eddie G," he said. "Come on in, man."

He backed away into the room, leaving the door open. I entered, expecting to find others in the room, but we were alone. I knew that Sammy usually traveled with his friend Arthur Silber, Jr., who had met Sammy when he was fifteen, just a little younger than Sammy himself. Back then Silber—as Sammy called him—was the son of the man who managed the Will Maston Trio, Arthur Silber. Arthur Jr. was on salary, but in reality he and Sammy were best friends.

"Whataya think of this?" Sammy asked, as I closed the door. The room was a suite, but a much smaller suite than we had at the Sands in Vegas.

Sammy drew one of the guns left-handed, twirled it a few times, then returned it to the holster a bit awkwardly.

"I'm tryin' to get as good with my left hand as I am with my right."

He drew the right one, executed the same maneuvers and then returned it to the holster flawlessly.

"You should be makin' westerns, Sam," I said.

"We're gonna start shootin' one in a few months," he told me. "Me, Frank, Dean, Peter and Joey. It's called *Sergeants 3*. It's a western based on Rudyard Kipling's 'Gunga Din.' Frank's producing, from a W. R. Burnett script. I hope that will lead to some more westerns."

"Good luck."

He smiled at me.

"But there's not much call for a one-eyed black Jew in westerns these days," he admitted.

I didn't know what to say to that.

"Hey, where are my manners?" he asked. "Have a seat. Can I get you a drink?"

"Bourbon would be good."

"Comin' up. Rocks?"

"Is there any other way?"

He laughed, went to the bar and made us both drinks. I wasn't sure what he was having, but it was roughly the same color as mine.

"How's May?" I asked.

"Good," he said. "She stayed home this time. Her mom's there."

"And Silber?"

"Had some business in L.A.; I'm on my own."

"You seem to be keeping yourself occupied."

"These?" he asked, looking down at his holsters. "You'd think guns would get me into more trouble, wouldn't you? Actually, I do get out, but I'm watching my p's and q's while I'm here without May and Silber. Of course, I don't have the guys to get me into trouble."

"Frank is here."

"He's keepin' to himself," Sammy said. "Dean's at the Sands, isn't he?"

"End of the week."

"Maybe I'll come down and catch that."

"Joey's there," I said. "He's staying to see Dean."

"I'll have to talk to Frank. Maybe he'll want to go, too."

"Sammy," I said, "Frank thinks I might be of help to you."

Sammy put his drink down, then drew both guns and tried twirling them together. He almost dropped the left one, then holstered both.

"Eddie, I know what you did for Frank and Dean last year," he said. "I also know none of that got out to the press."

"I don't talk to the press, Sammy," I said. "That's not part of my job."

"Neither is helping any of us when we get into trouble."

I snorted and said, "Tell that to Jack Entratter."

"We both know Jack wouldn't have fired you if you'd refused to help Frank and Dean."

I almost snorted again, but stopped myself.

He took a moment to unbuckle the gun belt and set it aside on a chair, then picked up his drink and sat in another chair.

"Sam, are you asking me if I'll be discreet?"

"No, Eddie," Sammy said, "I'm asking if you'll keep your damned mouth shut."

Four

"I'VE GOT A SLIGHT PROBLEM," Sammy began.

That much I already knew, but I let Sammy get to it in his own time.

"There's a picture . . . a photo . . . floating around that could be . . . embarrassing to me."

"A photo."

"Yeah."

He sat there and waited. I didn't say a word.

"Frank was right about you," he said, then.

"What'd he say?"

"That you wouldn't ask any questions."

"Oh, I'll ask questions," I said, "when the time is right. Why don't you just go on?"

"Okay, here's the deal. The photo is not exactly floating around," he said, "it's in somebody's hands." He paused, took a drink. "This is the thing I can't get my head around. A year ago my house was broken into and some negatives were taken. They were from a certain roll of film."

"Wait, somebody broke in and stole one roll? That's it? Nothing else?"

"Nothin'," he said, "and I have some expensive equipment, jewelry, some cash—nothin' but this roll of film."

"Okay," I said, "go on."

"I've been waitin' since then for the other shoe to drop and, man, it just dropped. I'm being blackmailed. Either I buy the picture back or it goes to the newspapers."

"And have you already agreed to the buy?"

"Not yet," he said. "I'm waiting to hear from them again."

"Man or woman?"

"I don't know," he said. "I found a note here when I arrived."

"In your room?"

"No, waitin' for me at the desk."

"Still got it?"

"Sure."

He got up, walked to a sideboard, opened a drawer and took something out. He came back and handed me a regular white envelope. I took out a typewritten note and unfolded it. It read, "If you want the negative be prepared to pay for it. We'll contact you." There were no errors or misspellings.

I looked at him and he stared back. I decided not to ask if there was a photo in the envelope with the note. In all likelihood there was, and he'd removed it. I figured that was his prerogative.

I put the note back in the envelope and returned it to him.

"Are you gonna agree to buy it back?"

"If the negative really comes with it."

"And how will you know that?"

Sammy waved his arms helplessly.

"I guess when we buy the photo the negative should be with it."

"And what if they made another negative?"

He wiped his hand across his forehead and said, "I don't know, Eddie. I'm making this up as I go along."

"So what do you want me to do, Sammy?" I asked. "Find out who the blackmailer is? Do you have any idea—"

"No, no," he said, cutting me off. "I know you're not a detective, Eddie. I just need a—you know, a go-between, I guess."

"So you want me to make the buy?"

"Yes."

I could do that, I thought. Didn't sound as dangerous as the other favors I'd done for Frank and Dean. No mob bosses or button men. Blackmailers didn't kill people, did they?

"Okay," I said, "I don't see why I can't do that."

"You sure?"

"Why not? How hard could it be?"

"I appreciate it, Eddie," Sammy said. "I really can't think of anyone else."

"Who else knows about this, Sammy?"

"Just you, me and Frank."

"That's it?"

"I haven't told Silber, or my dad or uncle," Sammy said. "I want to keep this as quiet as I can."

I could understand that even though I didn't know what was in the photo. I didn't need to know.

"Okay," I said. "You can count on me to keep it to myself."

I stood up, and he stood with me.

"So should I call you in Vegas when I hear," he asked, "or will you be staying in Tahoe?"

I looked at my watch. I didn't think it made any sense for me to go back. If I stayed and took Frank up on his offer of the cabin I might even be able to put in a few leisure hours. I hadn't had a vacation in a long time.

"I'll stay over, at least tonight," I said, as we walked to the door.

"I can get you a room here," he said.

"That's okay, Frank's giving me a cabin at the Cal Neva."

"Well then, at least let me leave a ticket at the door for tonight's performance."

"That I'll take you up on," I said. "I wouldn't miss a chance to see you on stage."

"I'll leave two," he promised. "Maybe you can get Frank to come, too."

"I'll tell him."

At the door he shook my hand warmly, then hugged me impulsively.

"I really appreciate this, Eddie."

"I haven't done anything yet, Sammy."

"I appreciate that you even came," he said. "Stop backstage tonight after the show."

"I will," I said. "See you then."

Five

I HAD THE DRIVER take me back to the Cal Neva.

"I need to get the key for cabin four from Mr. Sinatra," I told him.

"Here you go, sir." He reached back and handed me the key. "Mr. Sinatra says you should keep it."

"Frank knew I'd stay?" I asked.

"He hoped."

I took the key. When it came to these guys—Frank, Sammy, Dino—I guess I was pretty predictable.

Last year, in August, when they came to town to the premier of *Ocean's 11,* I had been feeling pretty foolish for thinking that they were my friends. After all, they were the Rat Pack and I was just a pit boss at the Sands. But since August they'd come to town—together and separately—and had always had time for a drink, or even dinner, and never failed to leave me show tickets. But this was really my first extended contact with Sammy. It remained to be seen if he and I would become friends.

On the way to the Cal Neva I asked Henry, "Is there someplace I can pick up a change of clothes?"

"There are clothes in the cabin, sir."

"He thought of that, too?"

Henry laughed.

"There are always clothes in the cabin, sir," he said. "All sizes. I'm sure you'll find something."

He dropped me off so I could walk to the cabin, but I decided to stop by cabin five, first. I knocked on the door and Frank answered. This time there was no book in his hand, just a drink.

"You back already? You get things straight with Smokey?"

"Pretty much," I said. "There's not much I can do until he hears something."

"You stayin' over or goin' back?"

I dangled the key from my finger and said, "Stayin'—big surprise to you."

He smiled, "I just took a chance, pally."

"Look, Sammy's leavin' tickets for us at the box office tonight for his show," I said. "Have you been to see him yet?"

"No," Frank said, "I've only been here a day or two myself. Sure, sure, let's go see him. He puts on a helluva show. I'll have Henry drive us, and then we can get some dinner with Charley."

Frank had nicknames for all his friends, but always called me Eddie, or Eddie G, or "pally." I wondered how he referred to me when I wasn't around?

"Catch a nap and a shower, or whatever," Frank said. "Swing by here around six and we'll go see Sam swing."

"Sounds good to me," I said.

There was no reason for me to go inside. As I turned to go down the stairs Frank closed the door.

I walked to my cabin and let myself in. The place was spotless. I knew that Frank had definite plans for the Cal Neva. I also knew that Dean was looking to get out, if he hadn't already. MoMo Giancana was not the owner of record, but he was the actual owner of the place. He had asked Frank, Dean and Skinny D'Amato to front for him and gave them all a percentage. Dean bought in on Frank's say-so, but when he found out that Giancana was at the top he decided to get out. I admired Dean because he never gave in to the mob boys. They didn't impress him, and they didn't scare him. He sang in their clubs—which they loved—but that was all he did, and he was paid well for it.

I checked the bar and found that Frank kept it fully stocked. I didn't flatter myself and think he'd done it for me. Not since Frank had told me this was the cabin all "the guys" used when they were in Tahoe. But I appreciated it, anyway.

I made myself a drink and carried it into the bedroom. I checked the dresser drawers and closets, found some things in my size, carried the drink into the bathroom with me, where I took a shower. By the time I had gotten dressed in the fresh clothes—all of which fit perfectly, down to the black loafers—I'd finished the drink. I went back to the bar and built another small one.

Refreshed, with nothing to do but wait to be picked up, I phoned Jack Entratter to let him know what was going on. Again, as in the past, I did not immediately tell him what Sammy's problem was. If it became necessary later, I would.

"So you're stayin' over?" he asked.

"Yeah, it doesn't make sense to come back now," I said. "Frank and me are goin' to Sammy's show, and then we're gonna have dinner."

"Life of leisure, huh?" he grunted.

"Hey, Jack, I'll forget all about it and come back if you want—"

"Naw, naw," Jack said, "settle down. Stay and come back tomorrow, or whenever Frank's done with you."

"It's Sammy I have to be concerned with—"

"Yeah, yeah, I know," Jack said, "but it's Frank who flew you up there."

When it came to the Rat Pack Jack would go out of his way for Dino or Sammy, but he'd walk on broken glass for Frank.

"Just keep me informed so I know if I have to replace you for any length of time."

"You got it, Jack."

"And, uh, tell Frank hello for me."

"I will."

I hung up and took the second drink to the window and looked out. It was quiet, nothing and no one moving. I thought back to last year, when I'd agreed to do two favors—one for Frank and one for Dean. On the surface neither had sounded dangerous, but both had heated up quickly. I'd been threatened, beaten, blown up, shot at—and after all of that, I was prepared to do it again. Why? Well, this didn't seem to have the same potential, but what did I know? I'd never dealt with blackmailers before.

No, I think it came down to how I felt about Frank and Dino. In the beginning I had liked the idea of being their friend. Okay, so I was a little starstruck. And between the filming of *Ocean's 11* and the release of it I came to think that they had used me. But since then, they had both kept in touch. I may have been deluding myself that these Hollywood big shots thought of me as a friend, but I thought of *them* as *my* friends, and I guess that was what counted.

I saw Henry walking up to my door. I set the glass down and went to the door to meet him.

Six

WATCHING SAMMY DAVIS JR. was an experience. That was the only way to describe it—and that wasn't me talking, that was Frank. He actually leaned over to me during the show and said those words to me.

Sammy sang, danced, played instruments, did impressions. Frank described himself as a "saloon singer." Sammy, he said, was an "entertainer."

At the halfway point Sammy took the time to talk to the audience, introduce the band, and then he pointed into the crowd.

"There's a very good friend of mine in the audience tonight. He *is* my friend, an amazing talent in his own right, the chairman of the board, the leader, Mr. Frank Sinatra, ladies and gentlemen."

Frank stood to thunderous applause, waved at Sammy and then sat back down.

"Do you like your seat, Frank?" Sammy asked. "Can you see okay?"

"I can see fine," Frank called out.

Sammy wiped his brow with his hand, as if Frank's reply gave him great relief.

"Gotta make sure Frank is comfortable, ladies and gentlemen," he said, milking the joke. "You never know who might come around later with Frank's complaint."

The audience laughed and Frank waved again and called out, "You're safe, Sam."

"Then let's get on with the show," Sammy said. "Here's a tune my friend Dino let me borrow. . . ."

"Hey, Eddie, man," Sammy said, shaking my hand as Frank and I entered his dressing room. "Sorry I didn't introduce you from the stage—"

"That's okay, Sam," I said. "What would you have told people about me?"

"Smokey," Frank said, giving Sammy a big hug, "you brought the house down, as usual. I'm tired just from watchin' you."

"Thanks for coming, Frank," Sammy said, returning the embrace.

"How's May?" Frank asked.

"She's good, Frank, good."

"You got enough energy left to go out and get somethin' to eat with us?" Frank asked.

"If we do it here in the hotel I do," Sammy said. "I'm not up for a big night out, Frank."

"Neither am I," I said.

"Yeah, okay," Frank said. "I'll take it easy on you two Clydes. How's the food here, Sam?"

"It's good, Frank."

"Good?"

Sammy smiled.

"It's okay. They'll feed us well. Hell, I remember the days when my dad, my uncle and me had to take our food out back and eat it at a picnic table behind the building."

"They treatin' you okay?" Frank asked.

"They're treating me fine, Frank," Sammy assured him, "just fine. Why don't you two get out of here and let me get dressed, and then we'll go and eat."

"Okay, Charley," Frank said, slapping Sammy on the shoulder. "Great show, as usual. Naw, even better than usual."

"Thanks, Frank," Sammy said. "That means a lot coming from you."

"Let's go, Eddie," Frank said. "We'll wait outside while Sam makes himself pretty."

I wanted to say, "That'll be a long wait," or something as funny, but I really didn't know how Sammy would take it. I wasn't *that* "in" yet, was I?

Seven

HAVING DINNER WITH FRANK AND SAMMY was a little like dining with Joey Bishop and Buddy Hackett. The two of them were very funny together, telling stories that had me in stitches. Other diners in the Harrah's Steak House stared over at us, putting their heads together and pointing. No one, however, walked over and interrupted us. There were stories about Frank and how he reacted to being interrupted in restaurants by autograph seekers. Apparently, the people in this restaurant had heard them.

Eventually the subject came around to the next Rat Pack movie, *Sergeants 3*. Frank, Dino and Peter were playing the soldiers, while Sammy had the Gunga Din part in this western spin-off of Kipling. Joey was apparently going to play a soldier who made life hard for the top three.

"Hey," Sammy said, at one point, "you think there's a part in the movie for Eddie, Frank?"

"Whataya think, pally?" Frank asked me. "Wanna be in a movie?"

I sat back, stunned.

"Just like that?" I asked. "I don't have any experience. Don't you have to check with somebody?"

"I don't have to check with anybody," Frank said. "Look, let me take a look at the script. I'll find something small for you. Whataya think of that?"

"Come on, Eddie," Sammy said. "It'll be a gas."

"I don't know what to say." It did sound like it could be fun, shooting a scene or two with these guys, but what if I got in way over my head?

"Come on, Eddie," Frank said. "It's got to be easier than some of the stuff you went through last year, and look how that turned out."

"I almost got killed."

"But you didn't," Frank said. "You came out on top, because that's what you do."

"Frank," Sammy said, "you're not forcing Eddie—"

I broke in before Frank could.

"He's not forcing me into anything, Sam," I said. "When I try to help you it's because I want to. Okay?"

"Okay," Sammy said.

"Sure it's okay," Frank said, putting one hand on my shoulder and the other on Sammy's. "We're all friends here, and friends help each other, right?"

Sammy and I agreed.

On our way out of the restaurant a husband and wife approached Sammy and Frank for an autograph. I had seen many demonstrations of the famed "Sinatra charm." In fact, I'd been subjected to it many times, but I had only had a glimpse—maybe even a glimmer—of the "Sinatra temper." As the couple approached us I was wondering if I was going to witness it, but instead both Frank and Sammy were charming and gracious and signed the autographs.

In the hotel lobby Frank gave Sammy another bone-crushing hug. I shook hands with Sammy and told him to call me as soon as he knew something.

"If I leave the Cal Neva, or Tahoe, I'll let you know where to find me."

"That's cool, Eddie," Sammy said. "Thanks."

Frank and I walked back outside to his car and Henry started back to the Cal Neva.

"Look at this place," Frank said. "First Harvey Gross opened his Wagon Wheel, then Bill Harrah came in and opened his place. For a few years there was a few casinos and ski lodges. Then last year the Winter Olympics came here, and now look at it. There's been an explosion here, Eddie. Now if your business is skiing or gambling you can come here and get a license to print your own money. It's a gold mine, and it's only gonna keep gettin' bigger."

He turned his head and looked at me.

"Do you know you can literally park in California and gamble in Nevada? We're actually in a place called Stateline, Nevada, although it's not considered a city, or even a town." He shook his head. "I can't figure out if this place is gonna eventually be overrun by gamblers, or skiers."

"I vote gamblers," I said.

"Why?"

"There's no gambling season."

Frank laughed and said, "That's a good point, Eddie."

Frank dropped me at my cabin and put his hand on my arm before I could get out of the car.

"I have to leave tomorrow," Frank said, "but I'll be back at the end of the week. I've got to talk to some architects."

"If I want to head back tomorrow? . . ."

"I'll leave the copter, and the pilot's phone number. Also, Henry will be here, in one of the cabins. Henry?"

"Cabin thirty, Mr. Sinatra."

"You've got my number in Palm Springs, right?" Frank asked me.

I had it. I'd never used it up to that point, but it was written in my phone book.

"Yes."

"Good, call me if anything comes up, otherwise I'll talk to you or Sammy at the end of the week."

"Gotcha."

"Look, Eddie, Sammy may only want you to be a go-between, but be careful. More than likely nothin'll go wrong, but . . ."

"If I learned anything last year, Frank, it's to be careful."

We shook hands and I said, "I'll see you, Frank."

"See ya, pally. Hang onto that key. Cabin's yours whenever you want it."

I got out and as I mounted the steps Henry pulled away. When I got to my door I saw a white envelope pinned to it.

I knew that already something had gone wrong.

Eight

I DROPPED THE NOTE on the table and said to Sammy, "This isn't right."

Sammy picked up the note, unfolded it and read it.

"How did they know?" he asked.

"That's my question."

He looked at it again then put it down.

"I don't get it," he said. "Only you, me and Frank knew you were going to help."

"And I only agreed yesterday," I said.

"I should call Frank—" he said, starting for the phone.

"No."

"Why not?"

"Because we can control this," I said. "Only you and I know about this. Let's keep it that way."

"But . . . we can trust Frank."

"Sammy who did you tell about this?"

"Only Frank."

"Nobody else?"

"I told you that yesterday," he said. "Only Frank."

"And we can trust Frank, right?"

"I thought . . . I thought we—" Sammy looked confused, then distressed.

"I'm not saying Frank gave it away," I told him, "not deliberately, anyway."

"Then what are you saying?"

"There's the driver, the copter pilot, his man George," I said, ticking them off on my fingers. "Who knows how many other people were around when he said something on the phone—"

"To who?"

"I don't know," I said. "Maybe Dean. I'm just making a point for us to keep this between ourselves. We can tell Frank that you were contacted, got a note with instructions. Just not where . . . not yet."

"Okay," he said, backing away from the phone. "So now what do we do?"

I walked to the table and picked up the note. Instructions were neatly typed.

"The meeting place is in Vegas," I said, "so the first thing I have to do is go back. Can you get your hands on this much money?"

"I can arrange for you to pick it up from a bank in Vegas. I can have Silber call—"

"Can you do it yourself, Sam?"

"You mean I can't even trust—"

"Just you and me for now, Sammy. Okay?"

"Well, okay," he said. "I'll make the call."

"I'll get Henry to take me to the helipad," I said. "Today's Tuesday and the meeting is set for Thursday. I want to get set up."

"Set up . . . how?"

"Well," I said, "all of a sudden I don't think I want to do this alone."

"But you just said, only you and me—"

"I know, but I think I have just the man for the job, and I'd only have to tell him so much."

"Who?"

"That's okay," I said. "I think I'll keep that little tidbit of information to myself."

I turned to leave.

"Where are you going?"

"Back to Vegas," I said. "I've got some arrangements to make, and a call. How long are you booked here for?"

"Until the end of next week."

"Good. I'll call you from Vegas."

"Call me when you get there," Sammy said. "And before you go to the meeting—and after."

"Sammy, relax," I said. "Concentrate on your shows. I'll take care of this."

"Eddie, wait," Sammy shouted as I opened the door.

He came up to me and said, "You're gonna have to look at the picture when you pay for it."

"That's right," I said. "How will I know it's the right one unless you tell me?"

"You'll know," Sammy said. "Just—yeah, you'll know when you see it. Just promise me something."

"What's that?"

"Don't show it to anyone else," he said. "Not anyone, under any circumstances, understand?"

"I understand, Sammy."

"Give me your word."

"I promise," I said. "No one sees that photo except me."

"Thanks, man," Sammy said. "You're solid."

"I'll talk to you, soon."

I went back to Henry and the car, waiting for me outside of Harrah's.

"Henry," I asked, "can you call the copter pilot and take me to the helipad? I want to get back to Vegas right away."

"We'll have to stop back at the Cal Neva, sir."

"You can call him from there?"

"He's also in one of the cabins. We'll just pick him up."

"Good man."

I sat back in the seat, took out the note and studied it again. The meet was set for a neighborhood that wasn't normally one I'd go to alone. Since somebody already knew I was the go-between, that just added to my trepidation about doing this alone.

Normally, I would have called my buddy Danny Bardini, a Las

Vegas private eye with an office on Fremont Street, but I knew Danny was out of town on a case. That left me with only one other option, one other person I felt I could trust.

I only hoped he'd be able to get to Vegas from New York on such short notice.

Nine

ALL DURING THE DRIVE to the helipad, and then the flight to Vegas, I kept wondering if either Henry or the copter pilot—"Skip"—had anything to do with the word leaking out? Then I had to wonder how much damage the leak might have done. Maybe Sammy should have switched to someone else, but it was too late to do anything about it.

When I got back to my house in Vegas I took a few minutes to shower and get a beer from the refrigerator. Then I sat down in my living room and made the phone call. I had to look the number up, because this was the first time I'd ever dialed it.

"Yeah?" the voice at the other end asked.

"Jerry?"

A pause, then, "Who wants ta know?"

"It's Eddie, Jerry," I said. "Eddie Gianelli, from Vegas."

"Hey, Mr. G.!" His tone changed completely. "Whataya say?"

I didn't know what to say. Exchange pleasantries with my friend, the Brooklyn hood? Or just tell him I needed his help? Wasn't I doing to him what I once thought Frank and Dino were doing to me? Just using me when it was convenient?

"How you doin', Jerry?"

"Good, Mr. G., good. How's the Caddy?"

"Safe and sound, buddy."

"I love drivin' that car, ya know?"

"Yeah, I do know, Jerry," I said. "How'd you like to drive it again?"

"Sure. When?"

"How's tomorrow?"

Now there was a long pause.

"Whataya sayin', Mr. G.? Ya need my help?"

"I guess that's what I'm sayin', Jerry," I admitted. "I've got a situation, here."

"This have to do with Mr. S.?"

"Yeah, it does, kind of."

"Tell me about it."

So I did. I told him everything except where we found the note with the instructions and what Sammy was buying. Actually, that second one wasn't hard, because I didn't really know what Sammy was buying.

"Sounds like there's a fink somewheres," Jerry said.

"That's what I was thinkin'," I said. "I was gonna ask Danny to go with me, but he's out of town—"

"You don't need the keyhole peeper, Mr. G.," Jerry said, "ya got me. When does this exchange gotta take place?"

"Thursday night," I said. "Can you get here by Thursday?"

"Mr. G.," Jerry said, "that's me on the next plane ta Vegas. . . ."

I called work and did a late shift in the pit at the Sands. I thought I was too late to see Jack Entratter, but in he walked just a little after midnight. Jack didn't usually stop to talk to individual pit bosses, but he and I had kind of a different relationship—especially since I'd started doing favors for Frank, Dean and the guys. And after the most recent one, last year, I think even MoMo Giancana ended up kind of liking me.

So if Frank and MoMo liked me, I was in even more with Jack.

"Hey, kid," he said, "I heard you were back."

He meant back in the pit, not back in Vegas. He already knew that.

"Can't stay away," I said. "Oh, by the way, I'll need Thursday off."

"This got anything to do with Sammy?" he asked.

"Yes."

When I didn't go any further he said, "Ah hell, okay. I'll get somebody to fill in for you."

"Thanks."

He walked away, then turned and said, "You're not gonna find any bodies this time, are you?"

"I hope not."

He gave me the eye. "That doesn't sound very encouraging."

"Oh, I'll need a room tomorrow."

"For who?"

"A friend of mine."

"You want a free room you're gonna have to tell me more than that."

"Jerry," I said.

"Lewis?" he asked, hopefully?

"Epstein."

"Him? Why's he comin' here?"

"I asked him to."

He walked back to me.

"Are you expecting trouble?"

"I . . . just want to make sure if there is trouble I'll be ready."

"And you wouldn't be ready alone?"

"I don't know," I said. "The last time . . . I'm not a detective, you know. Or a made guy. I don't carry a gun."

"Why would you need a gun?" he demanded. "What are you not tellin' me, Eddie?"

"Jack," I said, "I've told you all I can. I just want Jerry here for a little backup. Can I have a room?"

"Hell, kid, sure," he said. "It's just that guy—"

"What about him?"

"Trouble follows him."

"I don't see where he can be blamed for anything that happened in the past," I argued.

"Okay, then," Jack said, "it's the combination of you two. Trouble finds the two of you."

"That's not fair, either."

"Just watch your step," he said, "and your back. Okay?"

"Yeah, okay."

"I'll see you around," Jack said, and stalked off. He wasn't mad, he just always seemed to be stalking when he walked. Then again he always seemed kind of mad. It was probably because he was managing so many aspects of the Sands operation that he was always preoccupied with something.

I finished up my shift at 2 A.M. Normally I would've stayed 'til dawn, had breakfast and then gone home, but I had to be up early to pick Jerry up at the airport. I knew I'd have to get him settled in at the hotel, and then take him somewhere to satisfy what was the most prodigious appetite I'd ever run across—and in my thirteen years in Vegas I had seen a lot of appetites.

I satisfied my own appetite in the coffee shop before heading home to bed.

Ten

I ALMOST PULLED A MUSCLE trying to lift Jerry's single suitcase when we claimed it from the baggage check. He had told me he had only one bag because he "liked to travel light," but there was nothing light about it. Or small. But then there was nothing small about Jerry, either.

He was wearing lightweight gray slacks and a short-sleeved striped t-shirt that struggled to cover his torso and biceps. He was a big, thick, powerfully built man who might eventually go to fat with age. I figured with that thick center of gravity he had, he was probably more powerful than any muscle-bound bodybuilder.

"I'll take it, Mr. G.," he said, grabbing the suitcase one-handed from my two-handed grip and holding it easily.

Back then the McCarran Airport was one terminal, not much of a walk to the parking lot. People were rushing by us, though, to cars and cabs, in a hurry to get to a casino, and Jerry shook his head.

"I never saw people so anxious to lose their money than in this burg," he said.

"That's what this burg is for."

"That why you came here the first time?" he asked. "To lose money?"

"It wasn't my intention," I answered, "but that's the way it went down."

"Guess you was pretty smart to get on the other side, huh?"

"I wanted to live here," I told him, "and I couldn't have done that if I kept on gambling. So I got a job, and pretty soon I found out it wasn't the gambling I liked, it was just the overall atmosphere."

"Still pretty smart," he said.

When we got to the parking lot he easily installed his suitcase in the trunk of my Caddy and I tossed him the keys. He said he remembered the way to the strip, and we were off.

"You know, Mr. G.," he said, keeping his eye on the road, "I really think you coulda done this thing by yerself."

"You think so?"

"You handled yerself pretty well last year," he said, "both times."

"Why did you come, then?"

"Well, first, you asked me."

"And second?"

He tapped the steering wheel.

"I really wanted to drive your car again."

I got Jerry checked in, we dropped his bag in his room, and then went to the Garden Room.

"They gave me somethin' on the plane, but I'm starvin'," he said as we sat down.

A waitress came over and, since it wasn't yet noon, we ordered two steak-and-egg breakfasts. I'd only had a cup of coffee before leaving for the airport. She quickly brought us two cups, and a large orange juice for Jerry.

"Okay, Mr. G.," he said, "start from the beginning and tell me as much as you want to."

"Jerry, I can't—"

"I know you can't tell me everything," Jerry said. "I'm used ta that. Just tell me what I need ta know."

I'd almost forgotten that Jerry was much smarter than he usually let on.

I told him about going to dinner with Joey and Buddy Hackett, about Joey delivering Frank's message and my flying to Tahoe. The waitress came with our breakfasts and I gave him the rest while we ate.

"Yeah," he said, when I was done, "sounds like you got a rat on the inside somewhere, either somebody workin' for Mr. S. or somebody workin' for Mr. Davis." Then he peered across the table at me. "You ain't said nothin' to nobody, have you, Mr. G.?"

"Not a peep," I said. "I haven't even told you the whole story."

"I was just kiddin' around with you," he said. "I know you wouldn't let nothin' slip."

We had some coffee and Jerry had two pieces of apple pie.

"Are you full yet?" I asked.

"That should hold me for a while," he said. "So what do we do between now and the meet?"

I sat back.

"I've never done this before. Have you?"

"I ain't never made a blackmail payoff before," he said, "but I been to some meets."

"What did you do leading up to them?"

"I went and checked out the places that was picked," Jerry explained. "You never wanna walk into a situation like that blind."

"That sounds like a sound idea."

"And you wanna do it in the daylight," Jerry added, "because the meet's gonna take place at night."

"Well, why don't we go and do that right now?" I proposed.

"I drive?" he asked, brightening.

"Yep," I said, "you drive."

Eleven

JUST BLOCKS AWAY FROM the glitz and glamour of the Las Vegas strip the town can change drastically. Industrial Road is one of those streets. In fact, Jerry and I had already had an experience along that road, finding a body in a Dumpster while we were trying to find out who was threatening Dino last year.

"This looks familiar," Jerry said.

I told him and he nodded.

"This is in a different area, though," I said. "Much worse."

"I can see that," he said. As we drove along, the conditions worsened. Still warehouses and other businesses, but a lot of the "transactions" being done in parking lots and back alleys—you get my drift.

"Over there," I said. "Pull in."

Jerry turned into the parking lot and cut the engine. We were looking at an abandoned warehouse with a large, crumbling parking lot and an open field behind it. There were some rusted out Dumpsters, but not much else in the way of cover. There were also plenty of beer cans and food wrappers against the walls.

"The roof," Jerry said.

"What?"

"If they get here first they can put somebody on the roof."

"Like . . . with a rifle?"

"That's what I mean."

"But why?" I asked. "We're just makin' an exchange, right?"

"As far as anybody knows," Jerry said, "but Mr. G., these people are gonna be careful. They don't know if you're gonna show up with the cops."

"You know," I said, "I may be too naïve for this stuff."

"You live in Vegas," Jerry said. "You ain't naïve, you just ain't had all the good kicked outta ya yet."

"I've been here thirteen years."

Jerry shrugged.

"Maybe you had a lotta good in you." He slapped me on the back. "But don't worry, we'll make a thug outta you, yet."

"So what do we do?" I asked. "We're going to be out in the open here."

"Not we," he said, "you."

"But I asked you here to . . . to back me up."

"I can watch your back without bein' out in the open with you," he said.

"So what do you suggest we do?"

"The meeting is set for after dark," he said. "There are no lights here, so they're probably counting on car lights—yours and theirs. You'll have to drop me further down the street and I'll come the rest of the way on foot."

"What about the trunk?" I asked. "You could be in the trunk."

"Even your car doesn't have a trunk big enough for me," he said. "Besides, they might check it."

"So where will you be?"

"Out there." He pointed to the field behind the parking lot.

"In the open?"

"In the open in the dark," he said. "They won't see me."

"What about the moon?"

"That's a chance I'll take," he said. "What's the moon been like, lately?"

I had to admit that I hadn't noticed.

"Well," Jerry said, "we'll know before we come out here."

"What if they get here first?"

"They will," he said, "but like I said, they'll have a man on the roof, or in one of these Dumpsters, and he's gonna be watchin' you."

"So that's it?" I asked. "Now we just wait until tomorrow night?"

"We'll take a drive around the building," he said, turning the engine back on, "just to have a look."

He drove completely around the building and we spotted several ways in—a front door, a back door, and a loading dock door, all closed.

"What if they take me inside?" I asked.

"They've got no reason to do anything to you, as long as you show up with the money," Jerry said. "The only thing they might do is double-cross you and Mr. Davis by making copies of . . . of whatever it is you're tryin' to buy. So if they wanna take you inside, don't panic."

"Easy for you to say."

"You hungry?" Jerry asked. "I'm hungry."

"Sure, let's go," I said. "I know of a good diner right near here."

Twelve

"YOU KNOW," I said to Jerry when we reached the diner, "I think we spend half our time together with me watching you eat."

"You eat, too," Jerry said.

"Yeah, but you don't watch me," I said. "You're so intent on your food."

"And you don't pay attention to your food?"

"I pay attention to a really good meal," I said. "You pay attention to every meal."

He looked confused.

"But every meal is a good meal," he said.

"Come on," I said, opening the car door, "I'll buy you some fries."

"I love fries. . . ."

After Jerry had eaten his fill of fries—really good diner fries—we went back to the Sands.

"I've got some calls to make," I said.

"I can come with ya."

"I don't need you to watch my back, yet," I said. "You remember where the race book is?"

"Oh, yeah." His eyes lit up. "I remember."

"I'll meet you there."

"Okay, Mr. G.," he said.

We split up. I went to Jack Entratter's office to use his phone. His girl told me he wasn't there, but she let me sit at an empty desk. I called Sammy in Tahoe, first.

"I made the arrangements for the money, Eddie," Sammy said. He gave me the name of the bank and the man I should see when I got there.

"Have you heard anything else?" I asked.

"Not a peep," he said. "No calls, no notes."

"Okay, I'll be in touch."

"Thanks, man," Sammy said. "I know I'm in good hands."

I almost said, "I hope so," but didn't think that would go over real well.

After that I called Frank in Palm Springs and gave him a rundown.

"I'm glad you brought big Jerry into it, Eddie," he said. "He's a good man to have on your side."

"I know it, Frank."

"Listen, I'll be back in Tahoe on Friday, so I'm gonna fly to Vegas for Dino's show. Why don't you and Sam meet me there?"

"Fine by me, Frank."

"I'll talk to Sammy," he said. "See you then."

When I hung up, Jack's girl was waving me over to her desk.

"I'm not supposed to be taking your messages, you know," she said.

"Messages? From who?"

"Just one," she said. "And I only took it because it was Mr. Martin."

"Dino?"

"He'd like you to have dinner with him tonight, if you have the time."

"Dinner with Dean? Sure. I'll call him—"

"I'll return the message for you," she said. "The Garden Room okay?"

"No," I said, "I'll take him someplace off the premises."

"Our restaurants aren't good enough for you?"

"I'll call Dean—" I said, but she cut me off.

"No," she said, "I'd like to . . . please."

That was when I realized how much she wanted to talk to him again.

"I'll have a car out in front waiting for both of you," she said. "Just tell me what time?"

"I tell you what," I said. "Why don't you work that out with Dino and let me know, huh?"

Her face brightened and she said, "I'll call him back right now."

"You do that," I said. "Thanks for the phone."

I left her to her task and went to get Jerry out of the horse book. He was going to be disappointed my errands didn't take longer.

"Want me to come into the bank with you?" he asked, as we pulled up outside.

"That's okay," I said. "You can wait out here."

"How much money you pickin' up, anyway?" he asked as I got out of the car.

"Fifty grand."

"That's all?" Jerry asked. "I thought they'd ask for more."

Yeah, I thought, so did I.

When I came out of the bank I was carrying a brown manila envelope, slightly larger than a normal No. 10 white one, with fifty thousand-dollar bills in it. It was bound with a strong rubber band.

I got in the car and Jerry said, "That's it? Fifty G's?"

"This is it." I tucked it inside my jacket.

I'd been concerned about carrying all that money, but I had been thinking about hundred-dollar bills. Obviously, Sammy had been thinking bigger than I had. He had arranged for the thousand-dollar bills. The only time we dealt with bills that large at the Sands was when our "whales" came to town. The bigger players liked the larger bills.

Jerry simply shrugged and said, "I thought it'd be bigger."

Thirteen

WHEN WE GOT BACK to the Sands I told Jerry I was going to have dinner with Dean.

"So you're on your own . . . unless you want to come with us?"

"Nope," he said, "three's a crowd. Don't worry, I can occupy myself. Ain't too hard in this town."

"Okay, but stay out of trouble?"

"I always stay out of trouble, Mr. G.," he said. "Fact is, whenever I do get in trouble in Vegas it seems to be your fault."

He turned and walked away before I could respond.

I could have gone home to change my clothes, but decided I didn't want to make the extra drive. Instead I went into the employees' locker room, took a shower and changed into a suit I kept in my locker for these types of occasions.

Before leaving the locker room I called Jack's girl and asked her where I was supposed to meet Dean.

"He said he'd meet you out front, in the car, in twenty minutes," she said. "We didn't think he should stand in the lobby. He'd be too conspicuous and people would bother him."

"You both thought that, huh?"

"Yes," she said firmly, and hung up.

I checked my watch. I had ten minutes to get to the waiting car. Maybe I'd beat Dean there.

When I went out the front door there was a black sedan parked in front. The driver got out and opened the door for me. I recognized him, but didn't remember his name. He was apparently one of the drivers the Sands used for their guests.

As I slid into the back seat Dean smiled and said, "Hiya, pally."

We went to the Sahara, where I'd eaten with Joey and Buddy, in their Congo Room. As usual Frank's table was empty because he wasn't there, but the waiter recognized both Dean and me and gave the table to us.

"I hear Frank's in Tahoe," Dean said, as we sat. "Sammy, too."

"We're all going to be at your show on Friday night," I told him.

"That's great," Dino said. "I can drag those bums up on stage and make them do some of the work. But what do I do with you?"

"Just lay off me," I said. "I'm nobody, and there won't be anybody there who wants to hear about me."

Dean laughed and we gave our order to the waiter, who had seen it all and was not impressed.

Dean talked about his series of TV specials and said that some people wanted him to do it regularly.

"A weekly show would keep me from making my films and doing my act," he complained. "I'm not ready to settle into that grind."

"You'd be a huge hit on TV."

"You think so? It didn't work for Nat Cole, and Frank tried it twice. And they're great singers."

"You're a great singer, too, but they don't have what you have."

"And what's that?"

"Likability."

"Like a what?"

"People like you, Dean," I said.

"People like Frank," he argued. "And Nat."

"And Joey," I said. "And Sammy, too. But not the way they like you. It's just something that you have."

"And you think this . . . something . . . would come across on television?"

"I'm sure of it. Look what television did for Edd Byrnes."

"Kookie!" he said.

"Exactly. Television made him popular, because people liked him."

"Girls liked him."

"Women love you," I said, "and they'll love you more in their living rooms."

"You know," Dean said, leaning back and regarding me with interest, "you should come to work for me."

I laughed, then saw that he was serious.

"As what?"

"An advisor."

"What do I know about show business?"

"Look at what you just told me."

"That was common sense," I said. "An observation."

"Then I'll hire you to be my common sense."

"Dean—"

"Think about it, Eddie," Dean said, as the waiter arrived with our dinner. "That's all I ask. Give it some thought. It'd be nice to have someone with me who has no agenda."

"What about Mack?" I asked, referring to his man, Mack Gray, a majordomo type who had been passed on to him by George Raft.

"Okay," he said, "other than Mack."

Of course, there was a secret about Mack Gray I knew that I'd promised never to tell Dean, or he might have felt differently. Foolishly, Mack had sent Dean those threats early last year, hoping to make Dean more dependent on him. He'd seen the error of his ways, though, and I decided the best thing to do was keep Dean in the dark. I knew Mack loved Dean and would do anything for him, but I doubted he had much wisdom or common sense to pass on.

As the waiter set our plates down in front of us I said, "I'll think about it, Dean. Thanks."

"Then let's eat," he said. "I have a rehearsal tonight—although, if

Frank and Sammy are gonna be there opening night, there's not much chance anything will go as rehearsed."

We dug in, my mind reeling with the offer Dean had made me. I was flattered, to say the least, but I didn't think I was ready to leave Vegas just yet.

Fourteen

THE NEXT NIGHT I pulled the car into the parking lot on Industrial, butterflies in my stomach. Jerry was right, the only light was coming from my headlights. I stopped and kept the motor running and the lights on. I trusted that Jerry was out in the field in the dark, watching.

I checked my watch. I was five minutes early. Were blackmailers prompt? Apparently not, because I sat there for fifteen minutes and still nobody showed. I decided to drive around the building once, just in case they were on the other side and we were missing each other. No such luck. My once-around revealed I was alone in the parking lot. Were they inside? With no car in the lot? Maybe they had keys, opened the loading door, drove the car in and then went inside to wait? And if so, how was I supposed to know that? My note said to meet in the parking lot. On the seat next to me was a brown envelope with fifty grand inside.

I drove back around and stopped in my original position. I waited another twenty minutes, and then I jumped when somebody knocked on the window of the passenger side. When I saw it was Jerry I reached over and unlocked the door.

"They're not gonna show," he said, getting in. He picked up the envelope without curiosity and tossed it into the backseat.

"Why not?"

He shrugged.

"Maybe they saw me."

"Out there? How?"

He didn't answer.

"Maybe they're inside," Jerry said.

I told him what I was thinking about the loading dock door.

"Okay," he said, "let's take a look."

"Wait."

"For what?"

"We've been here before," I said. "What about the Dumpsters?"

"Oh yeah, that time we found that guy's body . . . you're thinkin' about those rusted-out Dumpsters over there?"

"Maybe somebody's hiding in one of them," I said.

"Or maybe there's a body," Jerry said. "Maybe the blackmailer had a sucker meet him here before us and somebody ended up in the Dumpster?"

"Yeah, maybe." I remembered Entratter warning me not to find any bodies this time. Also what he said about Jerry and I attracting trouble.

"Maybe we should just leave, Mr. G.," Jerry suggested.

It sounded like a good idea, except . . .

"What do I tell Sammy, then?"

"Tell him nobody showed up, and that you have to wait to be contacted again."

"Crap, crap, crap," I bitched, banging the steering wheel.

"Okay, point your headlights over there and I'll check the Dumpsters."

I turned the wheels and pulled forward so that my lights were illuminating the two Dumpsters.

"Wait here," he said, opening his door.

"No," I said, "I'll come with you."

"Did you bring a flashlight?" he asked.

"No."

He took one the size of a pen from his pocket and wiggled it at me, smiling.

We walked up to the Dumpsters and Jerry turned on his flashlight. We peered into one together, and then the other. Both were empty, except for beer cans, trash and puddles.

"There ya go," Jerry said. "No bodies. What about inside?"

"Are you . . . heeled?"

"Always."

"Okay," I said. "Let's go."

"Which door?"

"Let's start with the front."

We got back into the car and I maneuvered so that the front door was lit up. Jerry got out to try it, then got back in.

"Locked."

"Okay," I said. "Let's try the back."

I drove around and aimed the headlights at the back door, which was next to the loading dock door. I decided I wouldn't have minded if this one was also locked.

I got out of the car with Jerry, first sticking the money in my pocket. He grabbed the doorknob, pulled, and the door opened.

"Uh-oh." He looked at me. "We goin' in?"

"With just that little penlight?" I asked. "Let me move the car so the light's shining right inside."

I got in, maneuvered the car while Jerry directed me, then got out. It was a regular-size doorway, but as the light shone in the shaft widened.

"Let's go," I said.

"I'll go first," Jerry said, and took out his .45. With the gun in one hand and the penlight in the other, he stepped inside.

Fifteen

I FOLLOWED JERRY into the warehouse. We were blocking the car headlights from illuminating any part of the room. When Jerry moved aside I followed, and the beams came pouring in like a spotlight. The residual light from the spot lit some of the interior, but not all of it. There were still dark areas and corners. For that, Jerry started using his penlight.

"Looks completely empty," he said, and his voice echoed, as if to support his statement.

We walked around, the light from Jerry's flash showing the way. Here and there we found some rags, empty cardboard boxes, a puddle or two—and then something in a corner that looked like more rags, a large pile.

"Jerry . . ."

"You wanna leave, Mr. G.?" he asked. "Or wait outside?"

"No," I said, "we'll either stay together or go together."

"It's your call, then."

Backing out seemed the thing to do, but I said, "Let's take a look."

We moved closer to the pile and completely away from the light coming from the car. Now all we had was the thin shaft of light given off by Jerry's flashlight.

"Damn," I said, when he moved the light to reveal a head.

"Maybe it's a drunk, sleepin' it off," Jerry said.

He kicked, found something solid beneath the rags. He kicked again, then leaned down to take a closer look.

"Don't touch—" I started.

"I gotta touch to see if he's dead," he said. "Just his neck."

Jerry handed me his gun, then reached out and put two fingers to the man's neck.

"No pulse," he said. "He's dead."

"How?"

Jerry moved his light up and down the body.

"I can't see how he was killed, but he's dead, all right. And I ain't about to move these rags. I'm leavin' this guy just the way we found him."

He stood up, took the gun back and put it away. Then he shined the light on the corpse's face.

"Know 'im?"

The face being slack with death, I could only assume this guy had been in his thirties. He was dark-haired, with heavy black stubble. His eyes were closed, his thin-lipped mouth was hanging open.

"Never saw him before."

Jerry moved the light off the man's face.

"I guess we should call the police," I said.

"What for?"

"Well . . . we found a body."

"This body doesn't have to have anything to do with why we're here, Mr. G.," Jerry reasoned. "If we call the cops, we're right in the middle of it, and maybe we don't hafta be."

"So we just . . . walk out? What do I tell Sammy?"

"Tell him the truth," Jerry said. "What else is there to tell him? You guys'll just hafta wait to hear from the blackmailers again."

"And what do we tell them?"

"Also the truth," he said. "You gotta tell everybody the truth, with one exception."

"What's that?"

"The cops," Jerry said. "You don't never tell the truth to the cops.

It only gets ya in trouble. Nothin' good can happen if ya tell the cops the truth."

I thought a moment, then said, "I could call them anonymously."

"That's up to you, Mr. G.," Jerry said. "Right now I say we get the hell outta here. Your car's been sittin' in this parking lot with the lights on for too damn long as it is."

He was right about that. But still I didn't move. I just stood there staring down at the body.

"What?" Jerry asked.

"Let me have your light."

He handed it over.

"Whataya gonna do?"

"Just poke around a little bit," I said, crouching down. Using the tip of the light I poked into the rags that covered the body.

"Whataya lookin' for?"

"I just want to see if he has anything on him," I said.

"You think he's holdin' what you went after?" he asked.

"Could be."

I poked and prodded, hoping I wasn't completely screwing up any evidence. I didn't feel anything that could be an envelope. I didn't feel anything hard, or out of the ordinary. And then . . .

"What is it?" Jerry asked.

"I don't know." I felt it again, then tapped it. "Something hard, like metal."

"Are you curious enough to take a look?"

"Damn it, we're here," I said. "And maybe it's . . . something."

"Go ahead, then."

I used the penlight to move a couple of the rags, revealing what the metal thing was.

"That's a gun," Jerry said.

I moved the light up and down the weapon.

"Not just any gun," I said. "A six-gun."

"Like in John Wayne movies?"

"Yeah." Like the ones I had seen Sammy wearing in his room at Harrah's in Tahoe. "Great."

Jerry crouched down next to me, took the light and pushed aside some more rags. In for a penny, I thought . . .

"Okay," he said, "he was shot, maybe with this gun. See?"

I could see the hole in the guy's clothes, and the small amount of blood that had soaked his shirt.

"That's not much blood," I said.

"He died right away, so he didn't bleed out. We better get outta here."

"I want to take it with us."

"Take what?" He stood up. He was holding the light now and shone it in my face.

"The gun."

He studied my face with the light.

"You serious?"

"Yes."

"Why?"

"I'll explain it to you later."

Jerry looked around now, as if we were being watched, then back at me.

"You got a pen?" he asked.

"What?"

"A pen, do you got a pen on ya?"

"Yeah, but—"

"Use it to pick up the gun and let's get the hell outta here."

I took a pen out of my pocket, stuck it through the trigger guard and picked up the gun. Jerry reached down and, using his flashlight, moved the rags back to approximately where they were before we disturbed them. Then we hurried to the door, the gun swinging to and fro on my pen.

Sixteen

As WE DROVE AWAY he said, "We just fucked with evidence, ya know?"

"I know."

"I just wanted to make sure you knew what you was doin'."

"I know," I said, again.

"I heard Mr. Davis is pretty good with a six-gun," Jerry said, after a few more blocks.

"I heard that, too."

"That one of his?"

I turned and looked in the backseat, where I had tossed the gun.

"I don't know," I said, honestly.

"I guess we're gonna find out, huh?"

"I guess we are."

"So where we goin'?"

"Back to the Sands for now," I said. "I've got to make some calls."

When Jerry pulled the Caddy into the parking lot behind the Sands we sat there for a few minutes.

"We've got to put that gun somewhere," I said, jerking my head toward the backseat where I had tossed it and the envelope of money.

"Your trunk, for now," Jerry said.

"Isn't that the first place somebody would look?"

He shrugged.

"Who's lookin' now? I think it's pretty safe there for tonight. Nobody followed us back."

"If somebody knew I was gonna be there tonight, then they know where I work and live."

"So you think somebody left the gun there for you to find, just so they could take it back an hour later?" Jerry asked.

"No," I said, "more than likely the gun was left there for the cops to find."

"So you think you were sent there to find that body?"

"I was sent there to buy something," I said. "Instead, we found a body."

"You got stood up," Jerry said. "If we'd just left, ya wouldn't've found nothin'."

"But we went inside and did find something."

Jerry turned in the seat to face me.

"It's more than likely whoever was there to sell you the thing you was gonna buy had a fallin' out, and one of 'em got shot and left the other there, then took off."

"So the blackmailers fell out and . . . what? That's it?"

"If the one that's left still wants the money he'll make contact again."

I leaned my head back and closed my eyes.

"Hey, it'll be okay, Mr. G.," he said. "Nobody knows nothin'."

"I need a drink," I said. "You want a drink?"

"Sure."

"Let's go."

I got out of the Caddy and retrieved the gun and the envelope from the backseat. We opened the trunk and I put the gun—still holding it with the pen—underneath the spare. The envelope I put back in my pocket. Then we went inside to the Silver Queen Lounge and sat at the bar.

"Harry!" I called.

"Hey, Eddie. Hey, I know you, right?" Harry asked Jerry.

"Better if you didn't," Jerry said, and Harry nodded.

"Two bourbons, Harry," I said.

"Make mine a beer," Jerry said.

"Okay," I said, "two beers, and a bourbon."

"Comin' up."

"You okay, Mr. G.?" Jerry asked.

I held my hands out in front of me. They were shaking.

"Maybe not, Jerry."

"I'm tellin' ya," Jerry said. "It's gonna be fine."

"Yeah."

Harry came with the drinks and backed away quickly. I wondered what it would be like to be Jerry, able to scare people with my size, or a look.

I took a sip of bourbon and chased it down with a swallow of beer.

"Mr. G., you gonna call the cops?"

"I don't know yet," I said. "I'll have to talk to Sammy. He didn't want the cops involved."

"What about Mr. S.?"

"No," I said, shaking my head. "He won't have any input. It'll be up to Sammy."

Jerry shrugged and swallowed half his beer in one gulp.

"Jerry, you can occupy yourself tonight and tomorrow morning until I talk to Sammy."

"Where you goin'?"

"I'll go home and call him from there."

"I better come with you," Jerry said.

"Jerry, you've got a great room here, and the whole casino to keep you entertained."

"We found a dead body tonight, Mr. G.," Jerry said. "Somebody killed him. And that somebody is still out there."

"Well, like you said at the warehouse, we don't know that the killing has to do with the reason I was there."

"No, we don't," Jerry said, "but how much do you believe in coincidence?"

"Not much."

"So I better come with ya," he said. "You still got the same sofa? That sofa's pretty comfortable."

"Yeah," I said, "yeah, I've got the same sofa."

"Mr. G., I know I'm your second choice, here," the big man said. "I know you'd like to have yer buddy Bardini here. I may not figure out what's going on, but I won't let nothin' happen ta ya."

"I know that, Jerry," I said. "Believe me, I appreciate that you came when I called."

"Why wouldn't I, Mr. G.?"

Seventeen

I WAS TEMPTED TO TALK to Jack Entratter first, but two things stopped me. First, I would've had to wake him and second, I really did owe it to Sammy to call him. After all, I was sure he'd be waiting to hear what happened.

We collected Jerry's suitcase from his room and then drove to my house. I didn't bother checking him out of the hotel. I figured we might have use for his room later on.

When we got to the house he went to check out the kitchen while I called Sammy.

"Eddie, goddamn, man, I've been waiting for you to call."

"I know, Sammy, I'm sorry."

"How did things go?"

"Not the way anyone planned, I think."

"What do you mean?"

I told him the whole story, how nobody showed up and how we found a body inside the warehouse, shot to death.

"You had somebody with you?" he asked.

"Yeah, somebody I trust to watch my back," I answered, "but I didn't tell him why we were there. I mean, what we were supposed to be buying."

"What about this dead guy? Did you know him?"

"Never saw him before."

"Did you . . . I mean, I don't know what you do when you find a body. Did you . . . search him? Try to find out who he was?"

I lowered my voice and said, "I just did a quick search to see if he had the . . . object on him."

"And did he?"

"No," I said, "but he had something else."

"What?"

"A six-gun."

"A what?"

"A six-shooter, Sammy," I said. "Like the ones you had in your holster the other day."

"My guns are here, Eddie."

"Do you have any others, Sammy? At your house, maybe?"

"Well, yeah . . ."

"Can you call May and see if they're all there?"

"Aw, I don't want to do that, man," he said. "That'll just worry her."

"It would help us to know if this was one of your guns, Sammy," I said. "If it is then somebody tried to frame you for murder."

"Man," he said, "I was just tryin' to buy back a photo. Why would someone want to frame me?"

"I was gonna ask you that," I replied. "Look, I'll fly up there tomorrow and bring the gun."

"You took it?"

"Yeah," I said, "I couldn't leave it there."

"Eddie, man . . . you broke the law."

"I know, Sammy, I know, but if it was yours . . ."

"I don't know what to say, man," he said. "Thank you."

"Don't thank me yet," I said. "I'll be there early tomorrow, or as soon as I can get ahold of Frank's pilot."

"I'll call Frank first thing," he said. "I'll arrange it. A car will pick you up in the morning."

"Good, Sammy, good."

"Eddie . . . did you call the cops about the body?"

"No, Sam," I said, "not yet. I was going to but . . . let's wait until you look at the gun. If it's not yours, I can call the cops and report the body."

"And if it is mine?"

"I guess we'll have to cross that bridge when we come to it," I said. "I'll see you tomorrow."

As I hung up, Jerry yelled from the kitchen, "You got some baloney. You want a sandwich?"

"No thanks."

"I'm makin' coffee," he said.

"Good. I'll have some of that."

I left the phone and walked into the kitchen. Jerry had taken off his jacket, hung it over the back of a chair, and rolled up his sleeves. He was wearing his shoulder harness with his .45 under his left arm.

"You gotta stock your ice box with more stuff, Mr. G.," he said.

"Yeah, now that you're here, I'll have to."

"Geez, don't you eat?"

"I eat out, Jerry . . . a lot."

"Yeah, I know, but ya gotta have some food in the house, just in case."

"Just in case what?"

"Ya get hungry!"

"That's not a 'just in case' with you, Jerry," I said, "that's an 'all the time.'"

"Hey, I'm a big guy. I gotta eat." He bit into his baloney sandwich and licked a glob of mustard from the corner of his mouth. I didn't even know I had mustard. I never use it.

"So did you talk to Mr. Davis?"

"I did."

"What are we doin' tomorrow?"

"We're flyin' to Lake Tahoe in Frank's helicopter."

"Early, I bet."

"A car will pick us up and take us to the airport," I said.

"I'll get up and make some eggs," Jerry said. "I noticed you have eggs."

I didn't bother to tell him not to make breakfast. I knew it would be no use. Hell, if he had to eat I figured I might as well, too.

"I'll get you a pillow and some sheets for the sofa."

"Just a pillow's good, Mr. G." He patted the .45. "I got my baby to keep me warm."

I liked the idea of having Jerry on my sofa with his .45. Once last year a couple of goons had broken into my house and worked me over. Another time, two gunnies kicked in the door only to find Jerry there. And still another time somebody had blown up my Caddy, hoping to find me in it. After finding that body in the warehouse I probably wouldn't have slept in the house alone with no gun.

"I'm gonna turn in," I said. "I'll get up at the first smell of coffee."

"I'll get it goin' good an' early, Mr. G.," Jerry promised.

Eighteen

EVERYONE WHO TOOK US to Tahoe was the same—the driver who picked us up at the house, the helicopter pilot, and then Henry, who drove us from the heliport to Harrah's, rather than to the Cal Neva. I wasn't figuring we'd stay overnight.

When we got to Harrah's I considered making Jerry wait in the lobby, but if push came to shove Jerry's neck would be on the line along with mine. He deserved better.

I knocked on Sammy's door. When he opened it he looked as if he hadn't slept. His eyes were red-rimmed and he had a cigarette in his mouth—one of many I was sure he'd gone through since we talked the night before. I wondered if the red eyes were only from lack of sleep, or if he'd been drinking, as well. I didn't know Sammy's habits, if he drank or did drugs, so I couldn't really hazard a guess.

But he seemed steady as he said, "Come on in."

We followed him in and Jerry closed the door behind us.

"This the cat you told me about?" Sammy asked when we reached the sofa. "The one you said you could trust?"

"Yes," I said, "this is Jerry."

"I know you, don't I?" Sammy asked.

"Maybe," Jerry said. "I was around a couple of times last year."

"Sure, okay," Sammy said. "You helped with Frank and Dean's problems."

"I helped Mr. G., yeah."

Sammy leaned over, stubbed out the cigarette in a loaded ashtray, and immediately lit another one.

"You got it?" he asked, then. "You bring the gun?"

Jerry had offered to carry the gun and I'd let him. He was so big it made less of a bulge in his belt. He reached behind his back and took it out, wrapped in a cloth. Neither of us had touched it with our bare hands.

I put it down on the table and unwrapped it.

"Examine it without touching it," I told Sammy.

"I don't have to examine it," he said. "It's one of mine."

"How do you know?" I asked.

"A man knows his own guns," he said.

"He's right, Mr. G.," Jerry offered.

"That's just great," I said. "I need a drink. Anybody else?"

"Sure," Sammy said.

"I'll get 'em," Jerry said.

"Here." Sammy picked up a glass from the table next to the sofa and handed it to Jerry. "Bourbon, rocks."

"Me, too, Jerry."

Jerry went to the bar and built three drinks while I stayed where I was and watched Sammy, who actually crouched down and stared at the gun.

"Do we know for sure the cat was killed with this gun?" he asked.

"No," I said, "but it seems pretty obvious somebody wanted you to get the blame."

He used one finger to move the gun, just touching the cloth. Jerry came over, handed me my drink and put Sammy's down on the table.

"Is that gun registered to you?" I asked Sammy.

"No," he said, "none of them are registered. They're all supposed to be collector's pieces."

"Does that mean they're not supposed to fire?"

"Right," Sammy said. He grabbed his drink and stood up. "Most of them are plugged, like the two you saw yesterday."

"But this one actually works?"

"Yes."

"Who knew that?" I asked. "Who knows about your guns?"

"Just a few people," Sammy said, "but I trust them. May, Silber, my dad . . ."

There was an overstuffed armchair behind me and I decided to sit down. Jerry sat in an identical chair a few feet away. Sammy remained standing, drink in one hand, cigarette in the other, and it looked to me like he was swaying.

"Sam."

"Yeah?"

"Why don't you sit down?"

He stared at me for a moment, then seemed to process what I said and sat on the sofa.

"Somethin's wrong here," I said. "You're not tellin' me everything."

He hesitated.

"Come on, Sam. One of your guns goes missin' and you don't know it? I don't buy that."

"Okay," he said. "I'm sorry, man. Yeah, the gun was taken the same time the photos were."

"Why didn't you tell me?"

"I'm not sure I know the answer to that, Eddie," he replied. "Maybe I didn't think you'd help me if you knew about the gun."

"You never reported it missing?"

"I told you, none of them are registered."

I thought a minute, then said, "Okay. Forget it. It doesn't change anything right now. We still have to deal with this."

"You still haven't called the police?" Sammy asked.

"No," I said, "and as far as we know a body hasn't been found. At least, it wasn't on the news this morning."

"But you're gonna call 'em?"

I looked at Jerry, who looked away. I knew his thoughts on the subject.

"I feel like I have to."

"Of course."

"It's gonna be found sooner or later," I reasoned.

Sammy nodded, added another stubbed-out butt to the ashtray and lit up a fresh cigarette.

"What about this?" he asked. "What are we gonna do with this?"

We all stared at the gun.

"Well, it's yours." Jerry and I still hadn't touched it.

"But it may have killed someone."

"We don't know that, but yeah, it may have."

"Get rid of it," Jerry said.

Sammy and I both looked at him.

"Throw it in the lake."

Sammy looked at me.

"I do that, we'll never know," Sammy said.

"What's the difference?" I asked. "The guy's dead."

"If we throw away the murder weapon, how will they ever find out who the killer was?" he asked.

"If you don't get rid of it," Jerry said, "they could use it to prove you did it."

Sammy looked at me and I shrugged.

"Jerry knows more about this stuff than either one of us." I looked over at the big guy. "Keep going, Jerry."

"If the dead guy is one of the blackmailers," Jerry said, "who cares who killed 'im? You didn't, right?"

"Of course not," Sammy said. "I was here—I was on stage last night."

"We don't need an alibi, Sam," I said.

"It's more likely the blackmailers got into it and one of them shot the other one."

"So what do you suggest we do?" Sammy asked.

"Like I said, get rid of the gun," Jerry answered. "Then sit and wait for somebody to get in touch with you."

He sat back in his chair.

"He's more than just muscle, huh?" Sammy asked.

"And he can cook," I said.

Nineteen

I NEVER SHOULD HAVE said anything about Jerry being able to cook, because that reminded him that he was hungry. Again, true to his word, he had made breakfast for us earlier in Vegas. But several hours had passed, erasing all memory of a full stomach.

"When's the last time you ate?" I asked Sammy.

"I don't remember."

We called room service and ordered three full breakfasts and a pot of coffee. Jerry and I didn't finish our drinks, but Sammy did. In fact, booze was probably all he'd had since the night before.

"Sammy, why don't you go take a shower," I suggested. "By the time you come out the food'll be here."

"Yeah," Sammy said, rubbing one hand over his face. "Yeah, okay." He stubbed out the cigarette. "I'll be right back."

I hoped he wouldn't light another butt in the shower.

"We gonna stick around today?" Jerry asked.

"Might as well. They didn't get their money last night, so somebody'll probably make contact today, right?"

"I would."

I grabbed the three drink glasses, went to the bar, emptied Jerry's and mine into the sink, and left all of them there.

"He don't look so good, Mr. G.," Jerry said.

"I know. Let's see if we can get some food into him, and then maybe we can get him to lie down."

"We could slip him a mickey."

I stared at him. Did he just happen to have a pill in his pocket?

"Forget it," I said. "He's so tired he'll fall right to sleep."

"Or I could just give him a little love tap, ya know, to put 'im out?"

"No love taps on Sammy Davis Jr., Jerry," I said.

"Yeah, okay."

I sat back down and waited for either Sammy or room service, whichever came first.

"I don't hear a shower running," Jerry said.

"Maybe's it's too far away."

"This suite ain't that big."

"I better check."

I got up, went down the hall and into the bedroom. Sammy was lying on the bed, fast asleep. He'd never made it to the shower.

Jerry finished off both breakfasts before I finished mine.

"I think I'll call down for some sandwiches," I said. "That way Sammy can eat something when he gets up."

"Sandwiches are good," he said. "Get some extra."

I shook my head.

I called down and ordered the food, then hung up and walked to the window. There wasn't much to see. The suite's window overlooked the back parking lot.

"If the phone rings we're gonna have to wake him up," Jerry said.

"Maybe not," I said. "They know I was the go-between. They'll probably talk to me."

"Yeah, you're right."

Jerry gathered the plates and trays together so room service could take them away when they came with the sandwiches. I lifted the coffeepot and shook it. Maybe one cup left.

"You want some coffee?" I asked him.

"Naw, you have it."

Why do people do that, I wondered? Offer someone else the last of something when they really want it themselves? I poured myself the cup, glad that he'd turned it down.

When the sandwiches showed up they looked good—so good that Jerry asked, "Mind if I have one now?"

"Just leave one for Sammy," I said.

"No problem."

As the guy left with the tray from breakfast, I thought I should have ordered another pot of coffee.

"Jerry, any soft drinks behind the bar?"

"Some Coke, I think. You don't want another bourbon?" he asked.

"I didn't finish the first. Too early."

"I could mix it with the Coke."

"Bite your tongue."

I got a bottle of Coke from the fridge behind the bar and used the opener attached to the underside of the bar. Jerry and I got back in our chairs.

"So what's the plan?" he asked.

"We wait," I said, "for Sam to wake up, for the phone to ring, for a note to be delivered . . . we just wait."

"And if they don't make contact today?"

"We're going back to Vegas tonight," I said. "Sammy can call us."

"Call you about what?"

We looked up and saw Sammy walking into the room. He looked a little rested, and fresh from a shower, but he was still dragging.

"A new meeting place," I said. "If they don't call or make contact today. You got a show tonight, Sam?"

"No, not tonight," he said. "We're goin' to Dino's show tonight, right? With Frank?"

"I forgot about that," I admitted.

"I'll get dressed," Sammy said, "and we'll all go to Vegas."

"Slow down," I said. "Have a sandwich. We'll stick around here a while longer, give them a chance to call, and then we'll head to Vegas."

Sammy sat down on the sofa and accepted the sandwich Jerry retrieved from the fridge. He unwrapped it and took a bite.

"Anybody else want some coffee?" he asked, with his mouth full.

Twenty

NOBODY CALLED.

Nobody sent a note.

Nobody came to the door.

After Sammy called Frank at about 3 P.M. he told us, "Frank's gonna meet us at the Sands. We got a front table for Dino's show."

"Fine," I said. "We might as well get back."

"He got me a room at the Sands," Sammy said. "I'll change there. Where's the driver?"

"Waiting in the lobby, I hope."

"Call down and have him phone the helicopter pilot," Sammy said. "I'll be right with you, and then we can go."

I picked up the phone. Sammy started to leave the room, then turned and called to Jerry, "Hey, big fella, you wanna sit with us tonight?"

"With you, and Mr. G., and Mr. S.?" Jerry asked. "Sure."

"Good," Sammy said. "Joey'll be there, too. And he might bring Buddy. We'll make a party of it."

In a couple of hours Sammy's attitude seemed to have changed. I chose to look at that as a good thing. Maybe he needed to get out and party a little. Once he was contacted again it would start all over.

Jerry said, "What do we do with the gun?"

I looked at it, still lying on the cloth on the coffee table.

"Nobody's looking for it," I said.

"Not yet."

"When they find the body they'll start looking for a murder weapon," I said.

"We can't let 'em find it," Jerry said. "It'll point to Mr. Davis."

Just for a split second I thought, what if Sammy did it? We'd be covering up for him. But I didn't really think Sammy Davis Jr. was a killer.

"Mr. G.? Did you hear me?"

"No, Jerry," I said. "No, I didn't hear you. What did you say?"

"I said, why don't we drop it out of the helicopter? Over the desert, or the lake?"

I thought that over.

"Nobody would ever find it," he added.

"Maybe not," I said, "but the pilot would be a witness."

"Good point," Jerry said.

We both sat there, waiting for Sammy and staring at the gun. Then I remembered and called down to the lobby for the driver.

"There'll be three of us going to the heliport, Henry."

"Yes, sir. I'll be ready."

"Thank you, Henry."

When Sammy came out, Jerry and I were still wondering what to do with the gun.

"Why don't we just leave it here?" he suggested.

"We can't do that," I said.

"Why not?" Sammy asked. "Nobody's looking for it, nobody knows—"

"The blackmailers know," I said. "If this was an attempt to frame you they could call the cops and give them your name. What if they came here and found the gun?"

"Okay," Sammy said, "okay, so we just take it with us."

"I can carry it," Jerry offered.

"No," I said, "we have to hide it, or get rid of it."

"Okay," Sammy asked, "where?"

"That's what we've been trying to figure out."

* * *

We met Henry in the lobby.

"The car is ready, sir."

"Okay, Henry," I said. "Let's go."

Jerry, Sammy and I got in the backseat, and Henry headed for the heliport.

For a moment I thought about giving the gun to Henry to get rid of, but that would make him a witness—or, at least, an accomplice.

We had wrapped it back up in the hotel and Jerry carried it again now. When we got to Vegas we'd drive out to the desert and get rid of it, I thought, bury it. Bodies had been hidden in the desert for years without being found. Why not a hunk of metal?

"Let's just go to Vegas," I'd said in the room, "enjoy Dino's show, and worry about all of this tomorrow?"

"Sure," Sammy agreed, "why not? After all, maybe we'll never hear from them again. Maybe one killed the other and he's on the run."

Yeah, maybe, but what about the photo Sammy was afraid of?

What would happen to that?

Twenty-one

OUR TABLE WAS A RIOT, especially with Joey, Frank, Sammy and Buddy Hackett heckling Dino. At one point Dean pulled the four of them on stage with him and they cracked the entire audience up for a good twenty minutes while Jerry and I watched with everyone else. Then he kicked them off and we all fell quiet and listened to the man do what he did best—sing.

At one point he came out into the audience and approached a table where a young couple was sitting. They looked young enough to be newlywed, the man sandy-haired, the woman pretty and dark-haired.

"What's your name, sweetheart?" Dean asked her.

"Shirley," the girl said, shyly.

"And is this fine young man your husband?"

"Yes."

"What's his name?"

"Jerry."

"Where are you from, Shirley."

"San Francisco."

"Do you think your husband would mind if I sang a song to you?"

"I wouldn't care if he did," she said, and everyone laughed, including her husband.

"Well, all right, then . . ." Dean said, and he sang "I'd Cry Like a Baby," to her. She blushed furiously, but loved every moment of it. When he finished Dean shook hands with the beaming young husband and returned to the stage.

When he was finished with his act we all applauded, nobody louder or longer than Frank.

"Let's give him some time before we go backstage," Frank said.

I knew Frank was curious about how things were going, but he didn't mention it in front of Joey and Buddy. And I knew he wouldn't talk about it in front of Dino, either. He'd have to have the patience to wait until he got either me or Sammy alone.

We waited for the Copa Room to empty out and had one more round of drinks.

"You guys gotta let me come on stage with you one night," Buddy said.

"Where were you an hour ago, Buddy?" Frank asked. "You were up there with us."

"Just remember," Joey said, wagging his finger at Buddy, "there's only room for one comic in this act."

"Hey," Buddy said, "you start doin' some TV and there'll be room for me, right? Who else would you recommend?"

"I ain't recommending nobody, pal," Joey said, " 'cause I ain't givin' up this gig."

Frank looked at me and rolled his eyes. We both looked at Sammy, who seemed to be staring at something only he could see.

"Hey, Sam," Frank said, "wake up, baby. It's party time."

"I'm ready, Frank," Sammy said, with a big forced grin. He stubbed out a cigarette and lit another one right away.

"Come on," Frank said, pushing his chair back, "let's go back and see Dino."

"I'll get the check," I said, intending to have the Sands comp everybody.

"I already took care of it, pally," Frank said, slapping me on the shoulder. "Let's go."

Backstage was not as wild as it had been when the whole Rat Pack was entertaining, but it still took us a while to work through the crowd to where Dino was holding court.

"Just in time," he said, putting one arm around Frank and the other around Sammy. "I was goin' to change. Are we still on for tonight?"

"We sure are," Frank said. "It's been a while since we've all been together."

"Too bad Peter's not here, too," Sammy said.

"We don't need Peter," Frank said. "We got Eddie G."

I was flattered and figured that Peter's connection to the Kennedys was keeping him in Washington these days.

I knew that the real late-night swingers in the group were Frank and Sammy, but this was opening night for Dean, so everyone agreed to go out and celebrate.

We waited for Dean to change while the backstage area cleared out. Then when Sammy, Joey and Buddy left to go out front and wait, Frank grabbed my arm. Jerry drifted out with the other three and I knew he was feeling like a fifth—well, seventh—wheel.

"I know it's Sammy's business," Frank said to me, "but I haven't gotten a chance to get him alone. How's everything goin'?"

I hesitated, then decided that Sammy probably wouldn't mind Frank being clued in on some details.

"Not good, Frank."

I told Frank things didn't go well the first time I tried to help Sammy, so we were going to take a second shot at it. I didn't tell him about the photo, or the dead body. And I didn't tell him anything about Sammy's gun—which, by the way, Jerry said he'd taken care of.

After we'd landed in Vegas we dropped Sammy at the Sands so he could change, and then we went to my house so we could do the same. When we left the house I asked Jerry if he still had the gun on him. I was nervous about him getting caught carrying it. When he told me he didn't I was even more worried about it being found in my house.

"Don't worry," he said, "somebody would have to find it in more than one place. I broke it down in pieces and sort of . . . spread it around."

"Where did you put . . . You know what? I don't want to know."

Frank listened patiently. He knew he wasn't getting all of it, but in the end he just told me, "Keep tryin' to help him, Eddie. Sam's already been through a lot. You know, it ain't easy bein' black and Jewish. He takes a lot of crap."

"Don't worry, Frank," I assured him, "I'm doing my best."

"I know you are, Eddie," Frank said. "Listen, one other thing. Give big Jerry a pass tonight. I don't think he's real comfortable, but I also don't think he'd say so."

"I was having the same thought. I'll go out and talk to him now while you wait for Dean."

Frank nodded and I left. The Copa Room was empty and men were stacking chairs on top of the tables, so I went outside the front doors and found the guys waiting there. Joey and Buddy were arguing, or pretending to; Sammy's head rocked left and right, like he was watching a tennis tournament. Jerry was standing off to the side with no expression on his face. I walked over to him.

"Hey, Mr. G."

"Hey, Jerry," I said, "you look a little tired."

"Huh? Oh, I am, sorta—"

"Why don't you go up and use your room to get some rest?" I asked. "Or go back to the house."

"I'd hafta take the Caddy—"

"I'll get a ride," I assured him. "You don't have to come out with these bozos if you don't want to."

"I was kinda thinkin' about skippin' it. . . ."

"Sure, why not?" I said. "I'll see you later at the house."

"You sure you're gonna be okay?"

"These guys'll be around me all night, and like I said, I'll get a ride home."

"Well, okay," Jerry said, "but you be careful."

"Go ahead," I said, slapping him on one big shoulder. "Go home and get some rest."

"Thanks, Mr. G.," he said. "You'll, uh, explain to everybody—"

"Sure, sure," I said, "just go."

He looked very pleased at having been given his release—or else he was just looking forward to driving the Caddy again.

I turned and went to see what Joey and Buddy were beefing to each other about.

Twenty-two

WHILE I WAS OUT BOOZING and carousing with the boys, Jerry drove my Caddy back to my house. He said when he pulled into the driveway and cut the engine he could feel something was wrong. He didn't know how to explain it. It was some kind of extra sense—Jerry knew nothing about a "sixth sense" at that time—that had served him well over the years and kept him alive.

It was dark. He had pulled into the driveway with the lights on, and then cut them.

I didn't have a garage. At the time I bought the house I had managed to wrangle the price down because of that.

Jerry got out of the car, closed the door behind him, and stared at the house. The blinds on the front bay window were open, the way we had left them. He stared at the window, and then saw it. He must have spotted it out of the corner of his eye when he pulled in. A small pinpoint of light, like the glowing end of a cigarette when somebody draws on it.

Jerry had three choices: front door, back door, or get back in the car and leave. He had to decide fast, before whoever was inside decided to come out after him.

He moved around the car lazily, in no hurry, and when he was out of sight of the window he drew his gun and hurried around to the back. He didn't know what they'd do inside when he was out of sight. Maybe they'd come out to have a look. Or maybe they'd expect him to try the back.

He stopped at a side window, which he knew led to my bedroom. Jerry knew everything there was to know about my house. He made sure of that each of the other times he was there.

He hoped whoever was inside was watching the front and back doors, because he was going in through the bedroom. The locks on my window were for shit, which Jerry knew.

He jimmied the window open as quickly and quietly as he could, then climbed inside as silently as his bulk would allow him. At one point he feared his rear end had gotten wedged in the window, but then he slid through and was in the house.

Forty-five in hand he moved to the bedroom door. As he got closer to it and reached to pull it open, it suddenly slammed into him. He staggered back, kept hold of his gun, but there was a bright light in his face, blinding him.

"We're not that stupid, friend," a voice said. "Just drop the gun and let's talk."

We hit a few clubs, had some drinks and laughs, turned away many pretty ladies because it was "guy's night out." Eventually, we ended up at Frank's booth in the Congo Room at the Sahara. It was late, but they put out a spread for Frank and his guests. I was sorry I had sent Jerry home. He would have loved it.

"Time for me to call it a night," Dean announced.

"It's still early," Frank argued.

"I have to be on stage tomorrow night and do it all over again," Dean said, "and this time without you bums. I need my rest."

"Me, too, Frank," Sammy said. "I need to get back to Tahoe early tomorrow to get ready for tomorrow night's show."

"You guys are workaholics," Frank complained.

"Look at the pot callin' the kettle black," Dean said.

"What'd you say about black?" Sammy demanded.

"Oh no," Dean said, "I'm not starting a routine with you."

He stood up and put his hands on Frank's shoulders from behind.

"Thanks for coming to the show, Frank."

"You were great, Dino, as usual."

"Anybody want to share a limo?" he asked.

"Yeah, me," I said.

"Eddie!" Frank said, as if insulted.

"Sorry, Frank," I said, "but I've got things to do in the morning."

"I'll come along," Sammy said. He looked at Joey and Buddy. "I'll see you cats. If you get a chance come to Harrah's and catch my show."

"A capital idea, Sam," Buddy Hackett said.

"Capital," Joey agreed, and the two nodded at each other.

"Let's get another round of drinks, Frank," Buddy said.

"See?" Frank said to those of us who were leaving. "These are my real friends!"

Dean laughed, because he knew who Frank considered his real friends, and Sammy and I followed him outside.

"Goin' back to the Sands, Sammy?" Dean asked.

"I think I want to get some air," Sammy said. "Eddie, what are you gonna do?"

"I'm gonna get a ride to my house."

"I've never seen your pad," he said. "Mind if I tag along?"

"Sure, why not?"

We had been using two limos all night, so we all piled in one and left the other for Frank, Joey and Buddy. We dropped Dean off at the Sands first, and then had the driver take us to my house.

"Nice little neighborhood," Sammy said as we drove down my block.

"Right here," I said to the driver, and then suddenly I said, "no, keep goin'."

"What's the matter?" Sammy asked.

"Go to the corner," I said to the driver. To Sammy I said, "I'm not sure. Jerry's supposed to be there. My car's in the driveway, but there's no light in the house."

"Maybe he's asleep," Sammy said. "It's late."

It was 2 A.M.

"This is Vegas, Sammy," I said, "it's not that late."

"Okay, so what do you wanna do?" Sammy asked.

"I don't know."

"Call the police?"

"No," I said, "no cops."

"What's your name, driver?" Sammy asked.

"Thomas, Mr. Davis."

"Thomas, you got anything in the car we could use as a weapon?"

Thomas leaned forward, opened the glove compartment, and took out a wicked-looking automatic.

"Will this do?"

"Whoa," Sammy said, reaching for the gun. "A German Luger? This is groovy."

"I brought it back with me from Germany," Thomas said. I hadn't realized earlier that he was in his sixties.

"Do you have a permit for that?" I asked.

"Yes, sir."

"Can I borrow it?" Sammy asked.

"Sam," I said, "if you shoot somebody with that, not only are you gonna be in trouble, but so will Thomas."

"Oh, yeah," Sammy said, handing the gun back to the driver.

"You got a tire iron, or something?" I asked.

"If you gents are having a problem," Thomas said, "maybe me and my Luger can help?"

Twenty-three

THOMAS TURNED OUT to be ex-Army Ranger Sergeant Thomas Thorpe. Out of the fifteen million men and women who served in the armed forces during World War II, only three thousand were Rangers. They were trained for surprise attacks, many of which took place at night—like this.

"What would you like me to do, sir?" Thomas asked as we approached the house.

"I think I'll go in the front, Thomas, pretend there's nothing wrong. Why don't you go in the back—just in case something is wrong."

"Sounds good," he said.

"And me?" Sammy asked.

"I still think you should've stayed in the car, Sam."

"No way," Sammy said. "Whatever's goin' down is because of me. I want in."

I was holding a tire iron. As we reached my car I decided to put it down in the grass.

"What are you doin'?" Sammy asked.

"Well, if I'm gonna walk in like nothing's wrong I can't very well be carrying a tire iron, can I?"

"I suggest you put it down your pants leg," Thomas said. "You might need it."

I thought that over, then decided an Army Ranger knew what he was talking about. I picked the iron up and put it down my left pants leg. It didn't reach my knee, so I'd have no trouble walking.

"I would've offered to carry it," Sammy said with a grin, "but I've got short legs."

Thomas laughed, then started around the house.

"So we just walk in?" Sammy asked.

"If somebody's in there and they kill us they won't get any money out of you, will they?" I asked.

"Then why would they be in there?" Sam asked.

"Probably to deliver a message."

"For the next meeting?"

"Maybe."

"Well then let's go on in," Sammy said. "That's a message I'd like to get."

I took my keys out of my pocket and said, "Okay, let's go."

We walked up to the door. I put the key in, turned it, and twisted the knob. Just inside on the wall was a light switch. I hit it and the living room lit up.

Jerry was sitting in my armchair—or, rather, he was duct-taped to it. There was so much silver tape around him he looked like the tin man from *The Wizard of Oz*. His eyes appeared very calm, though.

There were two other men in the room: one standing, one seated on the sofa. They both held guns in their hands, sort of casually, not really pointed at us. That was all they had in common that I could see. The standing one was fat, with smooth, sweaty cheeks even though it wasn't that hot in the house. He looked young, like a big baby. The seated one was slender, with hollowed-out cheeks. He could've been anywhere from forty to fifty.

"Well, about time you came home," the seated one said. "And you brought a distinguished guest."

"That's Sammy Davis Jr.," the other man said. "Wow!"

"Thanks, man," Sammy said. "I'm flattered by the review."

I hoped neither of them noticed I was holding my left hand tight to my side so the tire iron wouldn't slide down.

"You okay Jerry?"

The big guy did his best to nod.

"Oh, he's fine," the seated man said. "We didn't hurt him none. We caught him comin' in the window of your bedroom. We thought maybe he was plannin' on stealin' somethin' so we decided to hold him for you. Maybe you wanna talk to him after we finish our business."

"And what business do we have?" I asked.

"I think you know," the man with the hollow cheeks said.

I looked at Sammy, who shrugged, playing it cool.

"I think you're gonna have to spell it out for us, pal," I said, "but first, why don't you two gents put the guns away?"

"These," Hollow Cheeks said, "are just a precaution. We didn't want you overreacting when you found us here."

"I'm a goddamned pit boss," I said. "How could I overreact? Ban you from the tables?"

Hollow Cheeks laughed, and the Big Baby took that as his cue to laugh as well. I looked beyond them through the kitchen door, wondering if Thomas was moving around in the dark.

"Hey, cats," Sammy said, "ain't your business with me?"

Big Baby slapped Hollow Cheeks on the shoulder and, grinning broadly, said, "Sammy Davis Jr.! Geez."

"Relax," said Hollow Cheeks, "don't get so excited over a little nigger."

I didn't know how that made Sammy feel, but it sure as hell pissed me off.

"Why don't you two bums get the hell out of my house?"

"Aw, did I say something to offend you?" Hollow Cheeks asked. "Or your little friend?"

"Just get to it," I said. "I want to cut my friend outta that tape."

"Oh, he's a friend of yours? Then he must've been coming through the window to do us some harm." He pointed the gun at Jerry. "Maybe I should take care of him."

"And maybe you should put the gun down, sir," Thomas said from the kitchen doorway.

"Benny?" Hollow Cheeks said.

Benny, the big baby, said, "Guy with a gun, Lee."

"Pointed at me?" He was looking at us, not the doorway.

"Yep."

Lee looked at me, keeping his gun pointed at Jerry.

"Looks like we got a Mexican standoff."

"I don't speak Spanish," I said. "You speak Spanish, Sammy?"

"Nada."

"Thomas?" I asked.

"A little German, but no Spanish, sir."

"Wise guy," Lee said.

"Put the gun down, state your business, and get out," I said.

"We only came to deliver a message," Lee said. "There's no reason for all this."

I knew if this turned into a shoot-out it would be a bloodbath I'd have to explain to the cops. If I came out of it alive.

"Then let's all put down the guns," I said.

"Your man first."

"Oh, no," I said. "My house, my rules. You and your buddy Benny first."

Lee seemed to be thinking it over.

"My friend Thomas is an ex–Army Ranger," I said. "He'll hardly miss from the doorway."

"You don't say," Lee said.

I looked over at the trussed-up Jerry and noticed that his eyes were just about popping out of their sockets. He was either having a seizure, or trying to tell me something.

"You may have a point," Lee said, then.

Jerry's eyes were jerking to the right, toward the front window. I looked over and saw a ripple in the drapes.

"Benny, let's put our guns down like the man said," Lee went on.

I drew the tire iron out of my pants—never thought I'd hear myself say or think that—and threw it with all my might at the drapes. It hit the man behind the drapes hard and he fell forward, face down on the floor, an ugly black revolver falling from his hand.

At that moment baby-faced Benny turned his gun on Thomas, who didn't hesitate. He fired once, and a hole appeared dead center in Benny's forehead.

Lee catapulted himself off the sofa. He seemed unsure about who to aim his gun at, although I don't know why. Thomas was the only one with a gun—that is, until Sammy reached down and scooped up the fallen black revolver.

Lee finally decided to turn his attention toward Thomas, who had dropped into a crouch. The shot Lee fired went over his head and into the wall. Sammy swiveled and fired at Lee, who was already moving again, so that Sammy's shot missed.

I dove across the room and threw myself on Jerry, to shield him from any flying bullets. Thomas took a bead on Lee and fired again. His Luger sent a bullet right into Lee's chest. Lee coughed, eyes bugging out. He said, "Wha—" and fell to the floor.

"Shit," I said. "How am I gonna explain this?"

Twenty-four

UNBELIEVABLY, THE MAN I hit with the tire iron was also dead. That meant we couldn't question any of them about why they were there.

"You hit him right in the head," Thomas said as he crouched over the body. "Split him open."

I was still unwinding duct tape from around Jerry. As I freed his mouth he told us what had happened when he returned home.

"I'm sorry, Mr. G.," he said. "I screwed up."

"There were three of them, Jerry," I said. "You should've just left."

He nodded. I knew his ego was battered, but we couldn't deal with that at the moment. I left him to finish freeing his legs.

Sammy was sitting on the sofa. He had dropped the revolver to the floor.

"I don't know what just happened here," he said. "Was this about my problem?"

"I don't know, Sam," I said. "We got three dead men who can't tell us a thing—four, if we count the one in the warehouse."

"There's another dead guy?" Thomas asked.

I looked at Sammy, who said, "Hey, he deserves to know something. He saved our asses."

Briefly, I told Thomas as little as possible while trying to make it seem like we were taking him into our confidence.

"I'm sorry you had to get involved in this," I ended, "but you probably saved all our lives."

"Are you planning to call the police?" he asked.

I looked around at Sammy, Jerry, the bodies on the floor, then back at Thomas.

"I don't know what we're gonna do," I said, honestly. "I guess since you're involved we'll have to call just to keep you out of trouble. I mean, there shouldn't be any trouble, since you fired in self-defense, and defense of all of us, but—"

"Since I saved all your lives can I ask a favor?" Thomas asked, cutting me off.

"Sure, go ahead."

"No cops."

"You got a reason?"

"Yes."

I waited then said, "A reason you can't share?"

"Not can't," he said. "Don't want to."

"Okay," I said, "I can respect that."

"Why isn't anyone bangin' on the door?" Sammy asked. "Quiet neighborhood like this?"

"If anybody heard shots, they don't know where they came from," Jerry said.

"They might call the cops anyway," Sammy offered.

We all stood silent for a moment.

"I don't hear any sirens," I said. "We've got time to talk this over."

"Man," Sammy said, "I'd rather not have cops involved, either."

Jerry was busy picking duct tape off his arms.

"Jerry?"

He looked up at me.

"Your call, Mr. G. I'll go along with anything you say. I'm uh, gonna go and try to wash this sticky stuff off."

He left the room. I walked over to the chair he'd been sitting in. The tape hadn't done it any good. I thought I might have to get rid of it.

I turned and looked at Sammy—still seated on the sofa—and Thomas—still standing over one of the bodies.

"You haven't called the cops about the first guy yet, have you?" Sammy asked.

"No."

"Well," Thomas said, "in for a penny . . ."

He was saying since I had already broken the law by not reporting that body, what were three more? Except that we were going to have to move these three.

I walked to the sofa—stepping over Lee—and sat next to Sammy. We listened, and there were still no sirens.

"Anybody decide anythin'?" Jerry asked, walking back into the room.

"Yeah," I said, "I think we need drinks all around, Jerry."

"Sure," he said. "I'll get 'em."

When we all had drinks in our hands—bourbon all around—I said, "If we don't report this we've got to get rid of the bodies."

"Coverin' up three killings, that's heavy," Jerry said. "Movin' the bodies, that's even heavier."

"I know, Jerry."

"I still prefer that to calling the police," Thomas said. "I'll help with anything you want to do."

I took a pull on my drink and sat back on the sofa. Next to me Sammy was sitting forward, one leg bouncing from either nerves or extra energy.

"Does anybody mind if Sammy leaves?" I asked.

"What?" Sammy said.

"I think you should get out of here, back to the Sands," I said. "Go back to Tahoe in the morning."

"I plan on going back," he said, "but I ain't leavin' here tonight. That'd be leavin' the three of you in the lurch."

"We can handle this, Mr. Davis," Jerry said.

"They're right," Thomas said. "You've got too much to lose, sir."

Sammy looked at the three of us in turn.

"I fired a gun, here," he said.

"You didn't hit anybody," I said.

"We'll wipe the gun down," Jerry said. "No prints."

"Thomas," I said, "can you drive Mr. Davis to the Sands? We don't want to involve a cab driver."

"Sure," Thomas said, "and then I'll come back and you fellas can tell me what we're going to do."

"Deal," I said.

Sammy stood up.

"I don't feel right about this."

"Sam," I said, "there's a possibility that what happened here had nothing to do with your problem."

"How likely is that?"

"Not likely," I agreed, "but possible. Why risk the publicity?"

He drained his drink and put the glass down on a nearby table.

"Okay," he said, "I'll leave, but—"

"No buts," I said. "I'll call you tomorrow. Whatever happened here, we still have your problem to consider."

"Maybe," he said, "everyone involved with that is dead right here in this room."

"These guys were messenger boys," Jerry said. "Not brains."

Sammy shrugged.

"I was just hopin'."

Twenty-five

Y EAH, I knew what I was doing could get me into a lot of trouble, but I also had to think about Sammy, and the poor driver, Thomas, who had no idea what he was getting into when he took that Luger out of his glove compartment. I remembered what Jerry said about nothing good coming from telling cops the truth. In this case he might've been right on the money.

After Thomas left to take Sammy to the Sands, Jerry and I had another drink.

"Thanks, Mr. G."

"For what? Gettin' you into this mess?"

"When the shootin' started you threw yerself on me," he said. "You coulda took a bullet for me. I won't forget that."

"I plead temporary insanity."

"I'm also real sorry."

"For what?"

"For lettin' those three bums get the jump on me when I thought I had the jump on them."

"Everybody makes mistakes, Jerry," I said. "I've made some big ones in the last few days, and I'm gettin' ready to make some more."

"Mr. G., this is all we can do," Jerry said. "The cops in this town don't like you and me. That one guy—Hargrove? He's bad news."

Hargrove was the detective Jerry and I had tangled with twice last year. Explaining all of this to him wouldn't be easy.

"The only way we're gonna stay out of trouble—and out of jail—is to get rid of these bodies."

I couldn't believe I was sitting in my living room with three dead guys on my floor, calmly talking about getting rid of them. I was wondering what was going to happen to me when it all sunk in.

"Okay," I said, with a heavy sigh, "where do we take them?"

"I don't know this burg like you do," he said. "City dump?"

"Too much of a cliché," I said. "Plus, somebody might stumble across them."

"Okay, so how about a junkyard?" he asked.

"Same problem."

"A lake?"

"That's a possibility, but . . ."

"Okay, whatayou suggest?"

"I do have an idea," I said, "but it's a little bit off the wall."

"What?"

"That warehouse."

"The one we found the other guy in?"

"Yeah," I said. "What if these guys killed him?"

"Then it would be, whatayacallit," he said, "ironical?"

"Yeah, it would be."

Jerry thought it over, nodding.

"The place is abandoned, might be a long time before they're found, and we can stage it so it looks like they all shot each other."

"That *would* be ironic," I said.

"It might not stand up to cops lookin' into it," Jerry said, "but by that time maybe we'll be done. You'll be back at work and I'll be back in New York."

I looked down at the three corpses. They had all bled into my rug. Damn.

"Yeah," Jerry said, "we're gonna have to clean your carpet."

Twenty-six

BY THE TIME Thomas returned—and I wasn't all that sure he would—we had the bodies wrapped in blankets. It took all the blankets I owned, and the rest of the duct tape, which the three men had brought with them. That made me think they might have been there to do more than just deliver a message.

"What's the plan?" he asked, as I let him in.

I told him.

"How do we get them there?"

"We'll need both cars," I said. "Yours and mine."

"Okay."

"You gonna get in trouble with your boss?"

He grinned and said, "I am my boss."

"Hey, man," Jerry said, approaching Thomas with his hand out, "I never said thanks."

They shook hands and Thomas said, "Don't mention it."

"I do got some bad news for you, though," Jerry added.

"What?"

"The Luger, we're gonna have ta leave it in the warehouse."

"Why?"

Jerry explained about setting the bodies up to look like they had all shot each other.

"How are you going to do that when one of them was killed with a tire iron?"

"Shit," I said. "We'll have to figure something out. Let's get 'em over there, first."

"The Caddy's got a big trunk," Jerry said. "I can back it up to the house. We take these bums out the back and drop them in the trunk. It's dark enough for nobody to see us."

"Okay," Thomas said. "After you move the Caddy I'll back my Chrysler up and we'll put the third body in there. After that I'll just follow you."

"Okay," I said with a queasy stomach, "let's do it."

Loading the bodies into the trunks was nervous work. Luckily I didn't live on a block with a lot of nighttime traffic. These were mostly people who went to work during the day and then came home at night, had dinner, and vegged out in front of the TV until bedtime.

Unloading them at the warehouse was not a problem. We pulled into the deserted parking lot, made our way to the back door, and then Jerry and I went inside to check if everything was the same. This time we brought a regular-sized flashlight from my house, and Thomas also had one in his trunk.

"Still there," Jerry said, as we looked down at the dead man. "And he's gettin' ripe."

It wasn't warm in the warehouse at the moment, but during the day it must have been like an oven. I had noticed the smell as we walked in.

"Let's get those others in here and scram."

With the help of Thomas we carried the three dead men in, unwrapped them, and laid them out in a way Jerry and I had worked out while we waited for Thomas at the house. There were certainly enough guns to go around.

And then we had the guy whose skull I had cracked.

"We can leave the tire iron behind," Jerry said. "Let them figure out how he was killed that way and not with a gun."

"So Thomas loses his tire iron, and his Luger," I said.

"Don't worry, Mr. Gianelli," Thomas said. "I lied about the gun. It's not registered to me, I didn't bring it back from the war. I bought it several years ago in a pawn shop."

"Why the lie?" I asked.

"It makes for a good story," the driver said. "I actually do have one I brought back from Germany, but I keep it in my house."

"And were you really a Ranger?"

"Oh yes," he said, "I wouldn't lie about that."

"Okay, then," I said. "All I have to do is buy you a new tire iron, and pay you for your time."

"The tire iron will be fine," Thomas said, as Jerry walked around making last minute adjustments. "You don't need to pay me anything. I've kinda enjoyed the evening."

"No, I've at least got to pay you what you would've got for drivin' us around all night."

"Mr. Sinatra paid me ahead of time."

"That's okay," I said. "We'll just add to it."

He shrugged and replied, "If you say so."

"I do."

"I think we got it," Jerry said, inspecting our work.

"I have a question," Thomas said.

"What?"

"Aren't the cops going to wonder how these men all killed each other in the dark?"

"Like I said," Jerry answered, "let 'em try ta figure it out. It'll keep them busy."

We left the warehouse and locked the door behind us. I wondered how long it would take me to get that smell out of my nostrils.

Twenty-seven

THOMAS ENDED UP TAKING the hundred-dollar bill I pushed into his hand and we parted company in the warehouse parking lot.

"That was odd," Jerry said, as we got into the Caddy.

"What was?"

"That guy," he said. "Comin' along when he did, doin' what he did . . . odd."

"What are you saying?"

Jerry shrugged and started the engine.

"I'm just sayin' it was odd."

When we got back to the house we still had work to do. We decided to leave the bloody blankets in the warehouse, among some cartons and tarps we found in a dark corner. Maybe the cops would never find them. But if they did, it'd just be another part of the puzzle for 'em to solve.

At the house, we had to clean the blood out of the living room rug. We also had to decide what to do with the chair Jerry had been duct-taped to.

It was well into the morning when we put away our buckets, sponges and mops. We had flushed gallons of bloody water down the toilet. I hoped to replace the products before my cleaning lady discovered they were gone. I also hoped the rug would dry before she showed up. I didn't want her asking any questions.

"I'm hungry," Jerry said, as first light started to brighten the interior of the house. "You hungry?"

"Yeah, I'm hungry, but I'm also tired," I said. "Let's go out and get something to eat and then come back and get some shut-eye."

"Fine with me."

We washed up, put on clean shirts—we'd been cleaning in our t-shirts—and left the house. There was a place not far from my house where Jerry and I had had breakfast a few times last year, and he remembered the way. He ordered a tall stack of pancakes while I went for eggs, bacon and the works.

"I can't believe I'm hungry after what we just did," I said.

Jerry leaned forward and lowered his voice, despite the fact that there was no one seated near us.

"Mr. G., we didn't shot nobody."

"I know it, but we broke a helluva lot of other laws," I said. "You may be used to that in New York, but I'm not."

"You and me bent a lot of 'em last year. Did ya lose sleep over those?"

"So I guess this is what happens when you start bendin' the laws," I reasoned. "Eventually, you end up breakin' 'em, too."

"Don't beat yerself up, Mr. G.," Jerry said. "You're doin' what you always do."

"What's that?"

"Tryin' ta help somebody. Ya kept Mr. Davis out of it."

"Sammy," I said, shaking my head. "I've got to call and tell him what's goin' on."

"Didn't he head back to Tahoe today?"

"You're right," I said. "I'll wait a while."

"Call him after ya get some sleep," Jerry suggested. "You don't look so good."

I didn't feel so good, either, but I was still hungry, so we dug in.

✳ ✳ ✳

When we came outside the sun was shining brightly and I thought about those four bodies inside that warehouse—one already partially ripe. I shaded my eyes.

"Back home?" Jerry asked.

"Only to get your things," I said. "I don't want to take a chance on somebody comin' to the house again. We'll catch some sleep at the Sands."

"I got two beds in my room, Mr. G.," Jerry said. "You're welcome to one."

"Thanks for the offer, Jerry," I said, "but I don't think I'll have any trouble getting myself a room."

"Naw, probably not," he said.

We drove from the diner to my block and as we started to pull in I saw the black-and-whites complete with flashing lights. Jerry stopped the car cold and we stared down the block.

"Cops!" he said, and in that one word you could hear his disdain.

"What the fuck—" I said.

"They're in front of your house."

"Jerry, get us out of here," I said, "and don't screech the tires."

"I'm way ahead of you, Mr. G."

Twenty-eight

WE HEADED FOR THE SANDS. If we had to, we could get lost there.

"How the hell did they know?" Jerry asked.

"I guess some neighbor did hear the shooting, after all."

"Then why did it take this long for them to come?" he asked. "The cops usually respond real fast to a call of shots fired." He seemed to think a moment, then said, "Shit, if they go inside—"

"—they'll find a recently cleaned living room rug, and nothing else."

He gave me a quick look, then turned his attention back to the road.

"What?" I asked.

"There's one thing we forgot, in all the hurryin' around, gettin' rid of the bodies an' cleaning up the blood."

"Forgot? What did we—oh crap." I remembered one of the men took a shot at Thomas while he stood in the kitchen doorway. "There's a bullet in the wall."

"Yes."

"Shit."

"Maybe they won't go inside," he offered. "Or maybe they weren't even in front of your house."

"You're right," I said. "Maybe Mr. Benson was beating his wife again."

The police did respond to the Benson home about once a month. I couldn't remember when the last time was.

"On the other hand," I said, "maybe somebody called the cops and told them what happened."

"Who would know that?"

"Whoever sent the messengers."

"But why would they do that? You're the go-between."

"Maybe they want another go-between," I said. "Maybe they've lost too many people as it is."

"Like I said before," Jerry said, "you ain't shot nobody."

"Maybe they don't know that. And maybe," I added, "we don't know what the hell is going on."

We parked behind the Sands and went inside. I felt like I was literally dragging my ass behind me.

"I'm gonna get some sleep," I said. "I suggest you do the same."

"What if the cops come lookin' for us?"

"Then they'll wake us up."

He went to the elevator court and I went to the front desk to get the key for one of the rooms kept for employees.

I knew the pretty young blonde behind the desk. Her name was Rose. She had a husband who worked at the Riviera, and she was a bit of a flirt.

"Do you have Mr. Entratter's okay for this, Eddie?" she asked, closing her hand into a fist with the room key inside.

"You can check with him if you like, Rose," I said.

"And what will you be using this room for?" she asked. "Entertaining one of your showgirls?"

"You know I only have eyes for you, Rose."

She smiled and said, "If only I didn't have a husband."

"My sentiments exactly."

She smiled broadly, batted her eyes at me, and handed the key over.

"I'm just gonna get some shut-eye."

"Sleep tight," she said, and then moved down the line to handle a check-in.

I hoped I would.

I slept more than tight; I slept like the dead for ten hours. I came awake slowly, rolling over and checking the clock, then looking around the room a few moments before I remembered where I was and what had happened. It was 9 P.M., not too late to call Sammy. In fact, I'd have to call him later, after he got off-stage. That was okay with me. My stomach was growling.

I'd gone to my locker for a fresh shirt and underwear before heading for the room. I'd just have to wear the same pants I wore the day before. That wasn't a problem. The shirt was a casual one, but since I wasn't working I didn't need a tie.

I turned the TV on as I dressed to see if there was anything on the news about bodies being found, or maybe even something about my block or my house. Thankfully, there was nothing—yet.

I left the room and went down to the Garden Room. When I got there it was no surprise that Jerry was already at a table, with a full dinner in front of him. I joined him.

"When did you get down here?" I asked.

"I just woke up half an hour ago, Mr. G.," he said. "And I woke up hungry."

"What a shock."

A waitress came over and I ordered a steak dinner, which was what Jerry was working on, and a beer.

"No cops," he said, around a huge chunk of meat.

"No," I said, "not yet."

"Maybe not at all."

"We can hope."

The waitress brought me a mug of beer.

"Thanks, Lucy."

"Sure, Mr. Gianelli."

"I forget you know everybody," he said.

"Lucy's been here a few months," I said. "She's putting herself through college."

"Pretty girl," he said. "You hittin' that?"

"There are a lot of pretty girls in Vegas, Jerry," I said. "One man can't hit 'em all."

He grinned and said, "You could try."

I sipped my beer, frowning as something he said hit me.

"You know, you're right."

"About what?"

"I do know a lot of people in this town," I said. "Maybe I should start using some of those contacts."

"To do what?"

"To find out what the hell is goin' on."

"That," he said, popping a potato into his mouth, "would be real helpful."

Twenty-nine

JERRY WENT TO WATCH the blackjack tables while I returned to my room to call Sammy. He was there, fresh from the stage. I asked him if he wanted to take a shower and wind down and I'd call him later.

"No, no," he said. "I wanna know what's goin' on."

"Have you heard from anyone?" I asked.

"Not a thing."

"Okay, we managed to do what we wanted to do last night," I said. "We, uh, got rid of all the dead weight."

"That's good . . . I think."

"Yeah, it is good, but we couldn't go back to the house. There was somethin' happenin' on the block. The police were there."

"At your house?"

"We're not sure," I said. "Could've been a domestic disturbance of some kind. Meanwhile, we're at the Sands. If you hear from anyone, call me here."

"Okay, Eddie."

"Listen, Sam . . ."

"Yeah?"

"There's a possibility that someone won't want me to be the go-between anymore."

"Well, that'll be tough," he said, "because I want you to."

"Okay, let's see what happens."

"Eddie, thanks, man. And tell the big cat I said thanks, too, will ya? And that other cool cat? You guys are the best."

"Talk to you soon, Sam."

I hung up and remained seated on the bed for a few moments, wondering what our next move should be.

I wondered if I should ask Sammy what this was all about. Just what was this photo he was trying to buy back, and why were people apparently dying over it? I was operating in the dark, and when it looked like all I had to do was make the buy, that was okay. But things were different now.

Another trip to Lake Tahoe might be in order.

But there were still some things I could do while we waited. As Jerry had pointed out, I knew a lot of people in Vegas. That was the original reason I'd been asked to help Frank and Dean last year.

Jerry and I were going to go out casino-hopping.

The last time Jerry had been in Vegas he'd discovered blackjack. He didn't play, but he loved to watch—mostly the people.

I found him studying a couple of tables that, at this time of night, were being played by tourists. The regulars usually came out during the day. Except for one. Ellie James was a woman of indeterminate age who had three kids, one grandchild, and still turned heads when she walked through the casino. Last year Jerry had noticed her and called her "the broad with the big titties."

"That broad still comin' in here?" he asked as I reached him.

"Ellie's here every day—or evening, that is. She comes in to play at night because she's busy during the day with her family."

"Oh, right." He frowned. "Still can't believe she's a grandma."

"Come on," I said. "We got some things to do."

"Like what?"

I started away and he fell into stride next to me.

"I'm gonna show you some other casinos, and we're gonna talk to some people"

"What people?"

"People who know what goes on in Vegas."

Thirty

OUR FIRST STOP was the Dunes. I knew a car jockey there who had two older brothers who worked dodges all over town. They were small time, but they had their fingers in lots of pies.

"Hey, Billy," I called as he started to get into a car.

"Hey, Eddie G.," Billy said, with a big grin. Billy Sykes had red hair and a face full of freckles that made him look sixteen, even though I knew he was thirty. His baby face made for even better tips. "What's shakin'?" He looked past me at Jerry. "Whoa, who's the man mountain?"

"Billy, this is Jerry," I said. "He's watchin' my back."

"Watchin' your—what's goin' on, Eddie? You in trouble?"

"A little bit," I said.

"What can I do?"

During the walk over I had been trying to think of a way of explaining my problem. I knew Billy wasn't the type who would ever talk to the police, but I also didn't want him connecting me to four dead bodies, if and when they showed up.

"I'm lookin' for somebody working a blackmail dodge," I said.

"Some high roller gettin' the squeeze?"

"Yeah, and he doesn't like it. He'd rather pay to find these guys than pay these guys."

"What's in it for me?"

"My gratitude," I said, "and a hundred bucks."

"Groovy," he said, then frowned. "You ain't thinkin' about my brothers, are ya? Their meat is usually tourists, not high rollers."

"No, I wasn't thinkin' about them, Billy, but maybe they heard somethin' helpful. They've always got their ears to the ground, right?"

"Hey, Billy, get that car out of here!" his boss yelled.

"I'll talk to 'em, Eddie, and I'll keep my ear to the ground," Billy promised. "I gotta get to work."

"Sure, Billy," I said. "Just call me at the Sands, okay?"

"Okay, Eddie."

Billy got in the car and drove it away.

"Can you trust that guy?" Jerry asked.

"I didn't really tell him anything," I said. "Even if those bodies show up, Billy will never connect them to me."

"What's next?" he asked.

"We were gonna walk up to the Stardust, but let's get the car. I wanna go downtown after that."

"Ain't we goin' inside?" Jerry pointed to the Dunes.

"No," I said, "but we'll go into the Stardust, and cross over to the Riv."

We got the Caddy and drove it over to the Stardust, parking behind it. We had to walk through the entire casino to get to where I wanted to go, the hotel lobby. I was hoping Gary Hogan was on the concierge's desk that night, and he was.

"That's our man," I said to Jerry.

"The mousy-lookin' bald guy?"

"That mousy-lookin' bald guy can get you anything you want in Vegas."

Gary looked up as we approached the desk. He'd been working the Vegas strip for years before I got there. He'd known everybody then and knew everybody now. In fact, he claimed that he was there the night Herb McDonald invented the buffet at the El Rancho Vegas.

"Hey, Eddie, man," Gary said, grinning. Though he was in his fifties his balding head was no sign of age. He told me once he'd gone bald in his thirties. "Who's your friend?"

"Gary Hogan, this is Jerry Epstein. Jerry's helping me out with something."

"Must be a big somethin'," Gary said. "Somethin' I can do?"

"Since you ask, yeah, there is."

"Need a big game?" he asked. "A girl? Two girls? Somethin' . . . kinkier?"

"Blackmail."

"You want to blackmail someone? I know a good photographer—"

"I thought maybe you might," I said, "but I'm kinda workin' for somebody on the other side of the play."

"Oh," Gary said. "So whataya need from me?"

"I need to know who in town works that kind of dodge—you know, with photos? Somebody not afraid to work a high-roller, high-profile type?"

"High profile? So you mean somebody with more balls than brains?"

"Right," I said, "and who doesn't work alone."

"Lemme give it some thought, Eddie," Gary said. "Maybe I'll have some ideas tomorrow."

"Thanks, Gary," I said. "You can get me at the Sands or leave a message anytime."

"Gotcha."

His phone rang then, as if on cue, and Jerry and I backed off and went out the front door.

We crossed over to the Riviera, where I had basically the same conversation with a bartender in the lounge. Pete Tynan had been tending bar in Vegas for twenty years, and had been at the Riv for three. He liked to spread his talents around. He either quit his jobs to go elsewhere, or ended up fired when he got caught sleeping with a guest.

I told him what I needed and he promised to give me a call if he thought of some names.

From the Riv we went back through the Stardust to retrieve the Caddy and drive downtown to the Golden Nugget.

"I hope this place got a new house dick," Jerry said, as we entered.

The old house dick had been killed the last time Jerry was in Vegas.

"I'm sure they've hired somebody, but I'm more interested in a woman who works here."

"Who's that?"

"Her name's Helen Jaye," I said. "She's the den mother to all the Golden Nugget showgirls."

"We gonna talk ta some showgirls?"

"We're going to talk to Helen," I said. "Chances are there'll be some showgirls around. Come on. Let's see how lucky we get."

Thirty-one

WE FOUND HELEN JAYE working with some of her girls in the Golden Nugget ballroom.

"... two, three, four!" she was saying as we walked in. "Can't anyone here count to four?"

"I can," I called out.

"Me, too," Jerry said.

Helen turned at the sound of our voices. She was getting ready to bite somebody's head off for interrupting her, but when she saw me she smiled.

Up to a few years ago Helen Jaye was still a headliner at the Golden Nugget, but she had retired at the top of her game to take the job of ramroding the girls instead of being one of them.

"Take ten, girls," she called, and came walking over to us. I knew she was in her mid-forties, but as far as I was concerned she could have still been performing as a headliner at any casino or club on the strip.

I knew some other ex-showgirls who were working the same kind of job—like Verna over at the Riviera, and Leelee at the Aladdin—but Helen was the best of 'em.

"Eddie G," she said, looking Jerry up and down, "you brought me a present."

Helen had a well-documented yen for big men.

"Jerry, meet Helen," I said.

"Hey, big fella," she said, batting her eyes at him, "you gonna be in town long?"

"Geez, I don't know—" Jerry started, but I cut him off.

"Leave him alone, Helen," I said. "He's got too much work to do."

"Yeah?" She took Jerry in like he was a six-and-a-half-foot ice cream cone and it was a very hot day. "Maybe some other time, huh?"

"Sure," he said.

Then she turned her attention to me.

"What can I do for you, Eddie?"

I knew that, in addition to handling the showgirls at the Golden Nugget, Helen ran some girls on the side. I didn't come right out and ask her to have her whores keep their ears open, but suggested in a roundabout way, which eventually got there.

"If I hear anything I'll sure let you know," she told me.

"I'd appreciate it, Helen."

"See ya around, big guy," she said to Jerry.

"Uh, yeah, sure . . ." Jerry said, and I pushed him out of there.

"Is that broad runnin' whores?" he asked, as we walked through the casino.

"Just a few," I said.

"What about her?" he asked. "She a whore?"

"Not that I know of," I said. "Why, you interested?"

"She's a good-lookin' broad," he said, "but a little too old for me, ya know?"

"What's wrong with a broad who's got a few miles on her?" I asked.

"Nothin'," he said, "but if I'm spendin' my dough, I like to spend it on young stuff, ya know?"

"Yeah, I do know, Jerry," I said. "And speakin' of young stuff, you just gave me an idea."

"What?"

"Come on."

We left the Golden Nugget and walked down the block to the

Fremont Casino. A young girl stood on the corner wearing short shorts and a flimsy top. She was also sporting some goose bumps, because it got cool in the desert at night. I knew she was legal, but she looked all of thirteen.

"Hey, Amy," I said.

"Eddie G," she said. "How's it hangin', handsome?"

She smiled at me with lips painted crimson and batted eyelashes that were caked with mascara.

I took hold of her elbow and walked her away from Jerry so I could whisper what I wanted in her ear. Nobody knew the streets like Amy, and I wanted her to keep her ears open. I pushed a twenty into her hand and she grinned, tucking it into her top. I'd say she put it between her breasts, but she didn't have any breasts to speak of.

"I'll let you know if I hear anything, Eddie," she promised.

"Good girl."

I walked over to where I'd left Jerry standing on the corner, and he said, "Now that's too young."

"She's nineteen."

"Yer kiddin'. She looks thirteen."

"That's what I think, but don't tell her that. She thinks she looks twelve."

We walked back down the block to the Nugget, wandering through it again to get to the parking lot.

Being on the street with Jerry, checking sources I hadn't checked in a while, I noticed my Brooklyn accent creeping back into my speech. I'd been away from New York a long time, hadn't been a CPA for a lot of years. Working at the Sands I always found myself adapting my speech patterns to whoever I was talking to at the time. When I was with Jack Entratter I became Brooklyn Eddie again, but with high rollers my speech smoothed out a bit. And with certain ladies.

"Where to now?" Jerry asked as we got into the car, with him in the driver's seat.

"Hm? Oh, just head back to the strip and I'll give it some thought."

* * *

"Pull over here," I said a few minutes later.

We were back on the strip, just outside of Wilbur Clark's Desert Inn.

"Hey, Andy!" I yelled.

A kid who looked and was twelve—refreshing, wasn't it?—came over to the car.

"Hey, Eddie G," he greeted. "Whatcher doin' in the passenger seat of yer own Caddy?"

"Got a friend of mine drivin' it," I said. "He appreciates good cars. Jerry, meet Andy."

"Hey, kid."

Andy leaned in, staring at the length of Jerry's legs.

"Wow. What's he go, about six-four?"

"Little bigger," I said.

"What can I do for ya, Eddie? I gotta pass out the rest of these flyers."

"I'm not going to interfere with your job, Andy. I just want you to stay alert for me."

"Why?"

I gave him the same story I had given the others.

"You doin' this for one of your whales?"

"That's right."

"Wouldn't be Mr. Sinatra, would it?" he asked, his eyes lighting up. "I'd really like to do somethin' for Mr. Sinatra, ya know?"

"Andy," I said, "I can honestly tell you this isn't for Mr. Sinatra."

"Well, okay, Eddie," the kid said, "I'll just have ta do it for you."

I handed the kid a sawbuck and said, "Thanks, Andy. I'll appreciate anything you can do."

"Here," Andy said, reaching across me, "you look like you ap-preciate a good piece of ass."

Jerry took the flyer and Andy backed away from the car.

"Phone numbers?" Jerry asked, looking at me. "He's handin' out phones numbers for whores?"

"It's all legal here, Jerry," I said. "Why not?"

Jerry thought that over a moment, then shrugged, folded the flyer and put it in his jacket pocket.

"Where to, Mr. G.?"

"Home, Jerry. The Sands."

Thirty-two

AFTER A FEW HOURS of running around the strip and downtown, Jerry and I went into the Silver Queen Lounge for a couple of cold ones. The bartender—a new guy named Richard—put a new bowl of peanuts on the bar in front of us.

"Whatever happened to that red-haired gal you were tappin' for a while?" Jerry asked.

"Beverly. She got a better offer. She left to get married."

"That's too bad."

"No, that's good for her," I said. "She had a kid who needed a father and I'm not the type to get married."

"I getcha." He popped a handful of nuts into his mouth. "We doin' anythin' else tonight?"

"No," I said, "I think I've had it. But we're gonna fly back up to Tahoe again tomorrow to see Sammy."

"Early start?"

"Yup."

He got off his stool.

"I think I'll go have a sandwich in my room and then turn in."

"Okay," I said. "I'll see you in the lobby in the morning . . . let's make it around nine A.M.?"

"Okay, Mr. G.," he said. "Good night."

I watched Jerry leave the lounge, then I turned back to the bar and signaled the new guy to bring me another beer.

"There ya go, Mr. Gianelli," Richard said, setting a frosty mug in front of me.

"Thanks."

"Um, there was somebody in here earlier, looking for you, sir."

"Don't call me 'sir' Richard," I said. "I'm not your boss."

"Yes, si—I mean, sure, okay."

"Who was it?"

"I don't know, just some guy," he said. "He came in, asked if you were around. When I told him I didn't know, he left."

I took a better look at Richard. He was a handsome guy in his early thirties who, I had heard, was drawing some extra female clientele into the lounge when he was on duty. He had blond hair, with a shock of it falling down over his forehead. I wondered if that was part of the appeal to women. My own hairline had begun to recede lately.

But I wasn't watching him to see how good *looking* he was. I wanted to study his eyes, decide if he had any smarts to him.

"What did he *look* like? This guy who came to inquire about my whereabouts?"

He smiled, almost shyly.

"I do really good describing women because I notice them more," he admitted. "This was just . . . a guy. Not tall, dark-haired . . ."

"Thin or fat?"

"Thin, but not skinny."

"When you say dark are we talkin' hair or skin? Or both?"

"Black hair, I mean," Richard said. "His skin was pale, I think."

"Have you ever seen him in here before?"

"I don't think so."

"Did you see where he went when he left?"

"Um, there was a blonde and a brunette at the bar tryin' to get my attention," he said. "I didn't see which way he went."

"Okay, Richard, thanks," I said.

"Sure thing, Mr. Gianelli."

"Eddie," I said, "it's just Eddie."

"I hear folks call you Eddie G," he commented.

"Yeah, sometimes."

"Okay, Eddie G," he said, "let me know if you need anything else."

"This'll do it," I said, indicating the beer. "Just let me have a check."

"Do you usually pay for drinks?"

"Kid," I answered, "I always pay for drinks. It's a rule."

"Your rule?"

I shook my head.

"House rule." It was a Jack Entratter rule. There was no reason any employee should drink for nothing, he always said.

He gave me my check, I paid it, leaving most of it on the bar, and I sipped some more beer.

I went out to the hotel lobby, to the desk. There were a guy and girl on duty. The girl was pretty, but I didn't know her. I knew the guy. His name was Anthony something. Early twenties, he had just come out of training for his job. Which was probably why he'd caught this late shift.

"Hey, Anthony."

"Hey, Mr. Gianelli."

"You got any messages for me?"

"Not that I know of," he said. "Caitlin, we got any messages for Mr. Gianelli?"

Caitlin turned her dark gaze on me, brushed a lock of auburn hair from her eyes and said, "Nope, I don't have anything. Sorry, Eddie."

Crap, she knew my name and I hadn't known hers. When had we met, I wondered? And why didn't I remember meeting a doll like her?

"Well, was anybody askin' for me? Maybe a guy, dark hair, pale skin?"

"Gee, I don't remember anybody like that," Anthony said.

"Me, neither," Caitlin said, coming closer. "I'm sorry."

"Hey," I said, "don't be sorry. I just heard a guy was lookin' for me in the lounge. I guess he didn't want to find me bad enough to ask out here. Thanks, both of you."

"Sure," Anthony said.

" 'Bye, Eddie."

I stopped in mid-turn, looked at her and said, "Good-night, Caitlin."

I wouldn't forget her name again.

Thirty-three

I WENT TO MY ROOM, thinking about the guy who'd been trying to find me. A gambler, maybe a regular who needed something from me? Or another man involved in the Sammy Davis Jr. fiasco.

That's what it had turned into, a fiasco. Four men dead, and I didn't know exactly what was going on. If Sammy was holding something back I was going to get it out of him tomorrow.

I undressed and got into bed. I found myself wondering what the cops had been doing on my block the night before and, if they were at my house, why they hadn't come to the Sands looking for me. My old friend—and I use the term very loosely—Detective Hargrove would love to get something on me. Maybe he was trying to make his case before coming for me.

I made a mental note to stop in and see Jack Entratter before heading to Tahoe the next morning. Which meant I was going to have to get up early so I could see Entratter and still meet Jerry in the lobby at nine. I picked up the phone and dialed.

"Front desk."

"Caitlin?"

"Yes."

"It's Eddie Gianelli."

"Oh, hello, Eddie." Was there was a warm tone in her voice or was I imagining it?

"What can I do for you?"

"I'd like an early wake-up call," I said. "Like . . . six."

"That doesn't give you much time to sleep," she said. "It's almost one."

"Five hours should be plenty," I said.

"Okay, then," she said. "A six A.M. wake-up call for Mr. Eddie G."

"Thank you, Caitlin."

"Don't mention it, Eddie."

I hung up, turned off the light, pulled the sheet up over me, and wondered again if I was messed up enough that I had met this girl and didn't remember?

I woke when there was a knock on the door. In a fog, I got to my feet, clad only in boxers, and went to the door. When I reached it I suddenly came awake and wondered if there were cops outside.

I looked out the peephole and, instead of a cop, I saw a girl.

Caitlin.

I opened the door a crack. "Caitlin."

"Good morning, Eddie," she said. A sweet smell came off her, as if she'd just recently put on some perfume. "I thought I'd personally deliver your wake-up call."

"Is it six already?"

"Yes, it is," she said. "Time to get up. Or . . ."

"Or what?" I asked.

She smiled enigmatically, making me wait, then said, "Or time to let me in."

"Wha—"

She pushed on the door abruptly, catching me by surprise, and I was forced back far enough for her to come in.

"Caitlin, I'm in my underwear. . . ."

"I know, Eddie," she said, "so I guess it's only fair that I get down to mine."

I couldn't believe my eyes as she unbuttoned the white blouse all the front desk girls were supposed to wear.

"Caitlin, what are you doing?"

"What does it look like I'm doing, Eddie?" she asked, removing her blouse to reveal firm, peach-sized breasts in a lacy white bra. "I'm waking you up."

We both looked down at the same time and saw that she certainly was.

Thirty-four

WHEN I WOKE UP for the second time, Caitlin was gone. I got into the shower but even when I made it cold the memory of her firm young breasts, smooth strong thighs and agile mouth made me hard again. Even feeling like a dirty old man—she was apparently almost twenty years younger than I was—couldn't make it go away.

"Damn," I said. I tried thinking about Jerry waiting for me in the lobby. Yup, that did it. I was able to get dressed after that.

I still had a half hour before meeting Jerry, so I detoured to Entratter's office. I knew Jack had a house on Charleston Boulevard, but he also had a suite at the Sands. If he slept in the suite he'd be in his office this early.

When I entered the outer office his girl wasn't there, but I could hear him banging around inside. As I walked in he slammed a desk drawer angrily.

"Good morning," I said.

"What's good about it?" He sat in his chair and leaned back. It creaked beneath his weight. "Whataya want, Eddie? You finished with Sammy's business yet?"

"No, not yet," I said. "In fact, I've got to go to Tahoe again today."

"You know," he said, "if I find out you're takin' advantage of the situation—"

"Fuck you, Jack," I said. "Call Frank and tell him Sammy needs to get himself a new boy. I've already been through enough shit—"

"Okay, okay, take it easy," he said, sitting forward. "Christ, kid, don't lose your temper with me."

"You know me better than to accuse me of any shit, Jack."

"You're right, Eddie," he said. "I do. I'm sorry. I got up on the wrong side of the bed this morning."

"Yeah," I said, grudgingly, "okay."

"Go ahead to Tahoe, do whatever you gotta do," he told me.

I got up to leave.

"Hey, kid."

I turned.

"What shit have you been through already?"

"Forget it," I said. "It's nothin'."

It was bad enough that Thomas, the driver, had knowledge of the bodies and where we'd hidden them. That made four of us: me, Thomas, Sammy and Jerry. Thomas wouldn't say a word because he had killed them in front of three witnesses. And the rest of us would stay dummied up.

There was no need to clue Entratter in.

Jerry said, "You're late," as I approached him in the lobby. "The limo's outside."

"Sorry," I said, "I got held up."

"What was her name?"

I looked at him sharply, then realized he didn't know anything, he was just kidding around.

"Very funny," I said. "Come on, let's go."

We left the Sands and got into the limo for the drive to the airport.

✳   ✳   ✳

During the drive I thought about Caitlin. My track record with broads was pretty good, but that didn't mean I was used to young chicks coming to my room, throwing themselves at me.

After we'd made love, once we were lying side by side on the bed, I had to ask.

"Have we ever—"

"No, Eddie," she said, turning toward me and putting her hand on my chest. "Never before, but maybe again?"

"Sure," I said, "soon."

"Soon?" she asked, sliding her hand down beneath the sheet, "or now?"

She took hold of me and, to her delight and my surprise, I was able to say, "Okay, now . . ."

"You have any breakfast?" Jerry asked, interrupting my thoughts.

"No," I said, "it's too early. You?"

"I had somethin' last night, and then again this mornin'," he said, happily. "I love this town. Twenty-four-hour room service."

Like a kid in a candy store.

Thirty-five

FROM THE HELIPAD NEAR the Cal Neva we went directly to Harrah's. I didn't know if Frank was in his cabin, or at home in Palm Springs, but my only concern at the moment was talking to Sammy.

I knocked on the door to his room and when he opened it I said, "Hey, Sam."

"Eddie, hey Jerry," he greeted. "Come on in. I was just having breakfast."

Jerry closed the door and we followed Sammy to the sofa and sat down in front of a tray of food.

"Pot of coffee here," he said. "Anybody want a cup?"

"No, thanks."

Jerry hesitated, then said, "No."

"You cats wanna fill me in while I eat?"

I told him about moving the bodies, and where to. Also about cleaning my house, but forgetting there was a bullet left in the wall.

"You still don't know if the cops went in your house or not?" he asked.

"No," I said, "but if they had I'd've expected them to come lookin' for me at the Sands."

"You're probably right. I haven't heard a thing yet, from anybody," he said. "Maybe they've given up?"

" 'Scuse me, Mr. Davis?" Jerry said. "I don't know all that much about what's goin' on, but if there's money involved I doubt the blackmailers would give up."

"But it looks like things have gone wrong in a big way," Sammy said.

"All that would do is make them ask for even more," Jerry suggested.

The fifty thousand Sammy had given me was hidden in a safe at the Sands. I wondered how quick he'd be able to put his hands on more. Even for somebody like Sammy Davis Jr. fifty grand is fifty grand.

"I see," Sammy said.

"Sammy," I said, "we need to talk—I mean, seriously talk."

"About what, Eddie?"

"About what's really goin' on," I said.

It took a lot for me to ask. Even though I counted Dean and Frank as friends, the starstruck aspect of our relationship hadn't gone away. It was even more so with Sammy. We were more acquaintances than friends at this point; I had tremendous respect for him as an entertainer, but this was a conversation that was going to have to take place man to man.

And I hoped I wasn't about to piss him off.

Thirty-six

SAMMY PUT DOWN HIS FORK. He finished chewing what was in his mouth before speaking.

"What are you sayin', Eddie?"

"I'm saying that there may have been some stuff before that was none of my business, but that's all changed now. Too many people are dead. What's goin' on, Sam?"

Sammy sat back on the sofa. He looked as if he was trying to decide how to play this. He could get angry and tell me to leave, or he could try telling the truth.

"I have this hobby," he said, finally.

Did I want to hear what his hobby was?

"What kinda hobby?" Jerry asked.

"Photography," Sammy said. "I like to take photos. It started when Jerry Lewis gave me a camera as a gift a few years ago. Then, when I was doing *Mr. Wonderful* in New York I met Milt Lewis and he taught me a little bit about the proper lighting, angles and such. I got to be pretty good at it."

Sammy stood up and began pacing.

"I started carrying cameras with me everywhere," he went on. "Taking pictures of everyone." He turned and looked at me. "I even have some shots of you, from last year."

That surprised me, because I never saw him with a camera.

"You got any pictures of me?" Jerry asked.

"No," Sammy said, "not you, big guy. Sorry."

"That's okay," Jerry said. "I don't like havin' my picture took."

"Are you serious?" Sammy asked. "Man, that's like bein' immortalized for all time. You get your picture taken it's like you'll look like that forever. Frozen in time. You know what I mean?"

I looked at Jerry, who was staring at Sammy with no expression on his face.

"I don't know if I want to always look like this," he said, finally.

Sammy stared at Jerry for a few seconds, then smiled, genuinely amused.

"I can dig you, man," he said, laughing. "I don't know if I wanna look like this forever, either."

They both looked at me.

"Hey," I said, "I like the way I look now."

Sammy and Jerry shrugged and then Sammy walked over to the window and stared out. I knew he could see the marquee with his name on it. I noticed driving in that underneath SAMMY DAVIS JR. they had added SPECIAL ADDED ATTRACTION LAURINDO ALMEIDA. I knew he was a Brazilian classical guitarist. Years later, in 1966, they'd make an album together, but who knew that then?

"Sam?"

"Hmm?" He looked at me over his shoulder. "Oh, hell, Eddie, to make a long story short, I took a picture that somebody wants to sell back to me."

"A picture of what?"

He turned and looked at me.

"I don't know."

"Come on, Sam—"

"I'm missing a roll of film," he said, "that has a picture that is . . . personally embarrassing. I'm trying to buy it back before it shows up in the papers. I don't really wanna say more about it, Eddie."

"So it's not one photo we're tryin' to buy back?"

"It's one photo I want," he said, "but there's twenty-four on the roll."

"What if they've developed the whole roll?"

"It's not actually a roll, it's an envelope with the negatives from that roll," Sammy said. "That's how they know they have something to sell."

I looked at Jerry.

"I'm lost, Mr. G. Wanna drink?"

"Sure, why not?" I asked. "This whole thing's got me drinkin' a lot earlier, these days."

"Bourbon?"

"Please."

"Mr. Davis?"

"Yes, thanks, Jerry."

Jerry went and built three bourbons in a moment that was definitely filled with déjà vu.

As he handed us our drinks I said, "Sammy, don't you know what else is on that roll?"

He sat back down on the sofa, so Jerry and I once again took our armchairs. I couldn't help thinking we were having our own summit, only without the Leader, Frank Sinatra.

"I know it's the envelope with the photo I want," he said, "the last one. I've been wracking my brain tryin' to remember what else is on it. . . ."

"Where was it taken from?"

"My home in L.A. I have a darkroom. I develop my own pictures."

"So somebody with access to your home took them?"

"Somebody broke in while we weren't home."

"And that was all they took?"

"Yeah, that envelope and the gun." He shook his head. "Like I told you before, I've been waitin' for one or both of them to come back and haunt me."

"Don't you . . . keep a file? Catalog your film?"

"I was starting to," he said, "but I hadn't gotten to all of them yet."

"You must know something. What year did you take the photos?"

"It was last year."

"And where did you take photos last year?"

"All over," he said. "Vegas, here, L.A., New York, Europe . . ."

"What kind of photo would be worth fifty grand?" I said aloud.

"It's a . . . candid shot. Like I said, personal."

"Candid?"

"I like to catch people . . . unaware."

"Like me?"

"Yes," he admitted, "most of the shots I took of you were candid, but . . ."

". . . but I'm certainly not worth fifty thousand dollars."

"Few people are."

"But most of the people you photograph are famous," I said. "Frank, Dino, Joey, Peter . . ."

". . . Jerry Lewis, Kim Novak, Nat Cole, Buddy Hackett, Tony Bennett, May—"

"And some, like me, who aren't entertainers?"

"Sometimes," he admitted.

"Businessmen?"

"Sure," he said, "producers, directors, money men—"

"Money men?"

"The men who put up the cash for movies, records—"

"Oh," I said, "I thought you meant . . . mob money men."

"I don't usually associate with mob money men," he said.

"But you have performed at clubs owned by the mob," I said. "The Copa, the Ambassador?"

"Well, yes—"

"And you took photos?"

"Yes."

"So there could be some candid shot of, say, MoMo Giancana on there?"

"I suppose . . ."

"Or . . ."

I stopped myself.

"Or what?"

"Just a thought," I said. "So many men have died already, and it can't be for your personal photo. There's got to be somethin' else on there. . . ."

"What's your thought?" Sammy asked.

"Last year, when you were all here for *Ocean's Eleven* . . . when JFK was here . . . did you take photos then?"

"Yes, but . . . I didn't take any shots of the President."

"Are you sure?"

"Positive." He said. "In fact, the Secret Service wouldn't let me, even though he wasn't president yet."

"Too bad."

"Why too bad?"

"Well, if you'd taken a photo of Kennedy when he was . . . enjoying himself . . ."

"Oh, I get you," Sammy said. "That would be worth a lot of bread."

"A lot," I repeated. "If that was what it was they would've asked for a hell of a lot more than fifty grand, don't you think?"

"Well, yeah, but . . ."

"But what?"

"If you're right," he pointed out, "they wouldn't be askin' for it from me, would they?"

Thirty-seven

WHEN JERRY AND I LEFT Sammy's room we walked down the hall to the elevator.

"Jerry, we can't talk about this when we're around other people," I said. "The drivers, the helicopter pilots . . . nobody."

"I getcha, Mr. G.," he said. "Mum's the word."

"That way we can control who else hears about this."

The elevator doors opened and we got in. There were two people already there—a man and a woman who weren't together—and we picked up a few more along the way. When we got to the main floor we let them get out first, then followed.

"Whataya think, Mr. G.?" he asked.

"I can't figure out how somebody knew to break into Sammy's house in the first place," I said. "If we could figure that out, we might get some answers."

"So how do we figure it out?"

"We'll have to think about it once we get back to Vegas," I said. "While we're in the car, and the copter, we'll talk about something else entirely."

"Like what?"

As we approached the limo I said, "Cars, women, sports . . . anything but what we've just been talking about."

Before we got into the car Jerry said, "You know what I think the photo might be?"

"What?"

"A naked picture of May Britt. That'd be somethin' Mr. Davis would pay to get back. Man, a picture of that blond babe with all that pale skin . . . She's kinda like Marilyn, ya know?"

I didn't say anything as we got into the car, but from the beginning I had been thinking the same thing. And then when Sammy said something about candid photos I was even more sure that was it.

I knew that May Britt had not made a film since she married Sammy Davis Jr. In fact, her film career would virtually end because of the marriage. I also knew, at the time this was all happening, she was about four months pregnant.

I could only wonder what they'd gone through to be together. But while the effects on her were obvious, the effects on Sammy were not. He must have been holding everything inside, where no one else could see. Where he could suffer alone.

We didn't talk about it again until we were in my room at the Sands.

Jerry sat on the bed and looked at me, then looked around.

"Can't you get yerself a swankier setup?"

"I guess we could go back to my house," I said. "If the cops were lookin' for me they would have come here by now."

"I guess."

"Then again, we might be safer here," I added. "After all, they obviously know where I live—whoever 'they' are."

"What's this?" Jerry asked.

"What?"

He picked up an envelope from the night table. It had my name written on the front. I grabbed it from his hand and stared at it.

"It's the same kinda envelope," I said, "and the same handwriting as the first note. The one stuck to my door in Tahoe."

"Another note."

I opened the envelope.

"It's instructions for the next meeting," I said.

"Where's the meet, this time?"

"Reno. After dark, again." I looked at him. "Why Reno?"

"To take you away from a place you know?" he asked.

"They could've said Tahoe, for that."

"Then maybe it's to take you someplace that they know."

I picked up the phone and called the front desk. I got a man I knew named Ted.

"Did anyone send anything up to my room?" I asked. "Like an envelope?"

"Nope," he said, "I don't have anything for you."

Ted's not the smartest kid on the block.

"No, Ted, there's already an envelope in my room," I said. "I want to know how it got here. Would you check with the bell captain, see if anyone brought it up?"

"Sure, Mr. Gianelli."

"And call me right back."

I hung up.

"What about the maid?" Jerry asked.

"Good thought." This time I called housekeeping and made the same request. Now we just had to wait for a call back.

I sat on the bed next to him.

"The only people we know of who know what's gone on are you, me, Sammy and that driver, Thomas."

"Whatever happened to him?"

"Nothing," I said. "He's still doing what he does, I guess. Driving."

"He's got somethin' on us, now."

"Yeah, but we've got more on him," I reminded him. "He killed those men."

"Well, two of 'em," Jerry said. "You killed the third."

"The point is we've got something on each other. And he doesn't know where we are right now. I'm trying to figure out how they got this envelope here."

"Has anybody been in this room but you?" he asked.

"Oh, Jesus," I said, closing my eyes.

"What?"

"Caitlin."

"Who's Caitlin?"

I looked at him and said, "Exactly. Who is Caitlin?"

Thirty-eight

I EXPLAINED, as briefly as possible, about Caitlin.

"You got laid?" he asked, breaking it down into even simpler terms.

"Yes," I said, "but I should have suspected something when she came to my room."

"Don't you, uh . . . I just thought you had a lot of, um . . ."

"I do okay with women, Jerry, but this girl is twenty-four years old," I said. "I really don't think she came to my room just because she had to have me."

"So you think she's part of the gang?"

"If there is a gang. There's one way to find out," I said.

I called down to the employment department and asked about Caitlin. I listened to the reply and hung up.

"She started working here as a trainee last week," I told Jerry. "She quit today." I slapped my forehead with the heel of my hand. "Jesus, I'm so stupid!"

"Hey, she was good-lookin', right?"

"Very."

"So, you're just a guy," he said. "She threw herself at ya. What were you supposed to do?"

"Be smart," I said. "I should have been smart and figured something was up."

"So she left you a note. If that's all she did, so what? You were waitin' for more contact, anyway."

"True," I said, "but why didn't I see it this morning?"

"Maybe you had your mind on somethin' . . . else."

"Yeah, yeah," I said, waving at him. "Okay, Caitlin's gone, but she did what she came to do, I guess."

"She probably coulda done it without fuckin' you," he said, "like . . . slidin' the note under the door?"

I stared at him.

"I ain't no genius, Mr. G.," he said, "but what I got is a lot of common sense."

"Yeah," I said, "you're right about that one. Okay, so we have to go to Reno."

"When?"

"Today," I said, "we go today."

Instead of calling Sammy to arrange for Frank's helicopter I called Jack Entratter.

"You need a chopper to take you to Reno?" he repeated into the phone. "For what?"

"I can't tell you that, Jack."

"Yeah, okay," he said. "I'll arrange it. And a car."

"Thanks. Half an hour?"

"You got it."

When I hung up Jerry asked, "Why didn't you call Mr. Davis?"

"I don't want him to know about this meet."

His eyes widened.

"You don't trust Mr. Davis?"

"I just want to keep it quiet this time," I said. "Just between us two."

"Okay," he said. "Just between us. Now what?"

"I'm gonna wash up and then we can go down and take the car to the airport."

He made a face. "The helicopter, again."

"It doesn't bother you to fly in a helicopter, does it?"

"It don't thrill me."

"You sure hid your feelings real well."

"Yeah," he admitted, "I'm good at that."

I dry-washed my face with my hands and said, "I just need to slap some cold water on my face and then we can go."

"I could use some water myself."

We took turns at the sink in the bathroom, then left the room.

That is, we started to leave the room. When I opened the door there were some men in the hall. One of them had his hand raised, as if he was getting ready to knock on the door.

"Mr. Gianelli," Detective Hargrove said. "Just the man I was looking for." Then he looked past me. "Oh, and look who's in town. If I had any doubts when I came up here they're gone now. Come on, boys. We're takin' a ride downtown."

I could see that the meet in Reno was now definitely in jeopardy.

Thirty-nine

THE DOOR TO THE INTERVIEW ROOM opened and Hargrove came walking in. I had been waiting almost two hours.

"Where's Jerry?" I asked. "What the fuck did you do with him?"

"Don't worry about your buddy," Hargrove said. "He's been through this plenty of times before."

"Did you put him in a cell?" I asked. "That ain't fair, ya know."

"You ever notice how your Brooklyn accent comes out when you're agitated?" he asked, seating himself across from me. "Or when you've spent a lot of time with that Jewish torpedo? Yeah, you're starting to sound like him."

"Actually, Detective, you have a way of bringin' the Brooklyn out in me."

"And you know what you bring out in me, Gianelli?" he asked. "The urge to put you away."

"For what?"

He opened a brown eight-by-ten envelope, took out four photos, and placed them in front of me. All four were dead men. One was the man we'd found in the warehouse, the other three were the men who were killed in my house. I hoped my face was expressionless.

"You know any of these men?"

I leaned forward, as if to take a better look.

"No," I answered, leaning back. "Should I?"

"You tell me."

"I thought I just did."

Hargrove reached across the table and reclaimed the photos, putting them back in the envelope.

"Your buddy Jerry's singin' like a songbird," he said.

"Yeah, right."

Hargrove had to smile.

"Yeah, even I didn't believe that one."

"What's this all about, Hargrove?" I asked. "I've got a living to make, you know?"

"So do I, Eddie," he said, "and I'm doin' it right now."

"When's the last time we saw each other?" I asked.

"What? I don't know, last year? In the summer."

"Really?" I asked. "Geez, you got some gray in your hair since then, don'tcha?"

He touched his head of coal black hair and said, "What the—I'm younger than you are, Eddie. What the hell are you talkin' about?"

"Hey," I replied, "I'm just sayin' . . ."

"Never mind." He dropped his hand from his hair.

"Besides, you're not that much younger than me, maybe a year or two—"

"I said never mind." The unmistakable scent of Sen-Sen breath mints came wafting across the table at me.

"Okay, okay," I said. "Don't get sore. You wanna tell me what I'm doin' here?"

"Four dead men, that's what you're doin' here."

"What about them?"

"We got a tip that you knew something about them."

"A tip? From who?"

"Unknown source."

"You puttin' a lot of credence in unknown sources these days?"

"Not exactly," he said, sitting back. "But when I heard your name, I thought I'd take an interest."

"Well, were they gamblers?"

"Not that I know of," he said. "Maybe."

"Then why would I be involved with them? My business is gamblers."

"Maybe they're mobbed up," Hargrove said.

"Why would that connect them to me?"

He lit a cigarette, then pointed at me. "Because you're mobbed up."

"I am not—"

"You work at the Sands," he said, "the mob owns the Sands, therefore you're mobbed up."

I could have continued to argue the point with him, but decided against it. I needed to find out if they'd been in my house.

"How'd you find me at the Sands?"

"We went to your house, you weren't there," Hargrove said. "So we tried the Sands. They told us at the front desk what room you were in."

"I hope you didn't leave my house unlocked."

"What do you take us for?" he asked. "We didn't even go inside."

"I just figured you must've kicked in the door."

"Why would we do that?" he asked, annoyed. "I'm not the law-breaker, Eddie. I leave that to you and your New York gunsel. What's he doin' in Vegas, anyway?"

"He comes to visit now and then."

"Really? And every time he comes to town somebody dies, huh?"

"Detective, I'll bet somebody dies every day."

"Sometimes more than one."

"Those four," I said, indicating the envelope on the desk. "How did they die?"

"Well," Hargrove said, "at first it looked like they shot each other, but the closer we looked the more we realized it was just set up to appear that way." He leaned forward and stared me in the eye. "By somebody who knew what they were doing."

"Well," I said, "that leaves me out, doesn't it?"

"Maybe," he said, "maybe not, but it's right up the gunsel's alley, ain't it?"

"Jerry's stuck with me the whole time he's been in Vegas," I said. "He's been my guest. He hasn't killed anyone."

On the face of it, that was very true. Jerry had not killed any of the four men.

Hargrove sat back in his chair, then stood up and said, "I'll be back. Can I have somebody bring you some coffee?"

"Sure, why not?" I said. "Might as well get somethin' for free while I'm here."

He laughed and said, "I'll send someone right in to take your order, Eddie."

He left. Was he going back to Jerry? How long was he going to let me stew this time?

Did we have any chance of getting to Reno tomorrow?

Forty

I HAD THREE CUPS OF COFFEE before Hargrove came back in and sat. He started right in as if he hadn't been gone an hour and a half.

"We've got a real odd situation on our hands, Eddie," he said. He took the four photos out again and laid them down in a row on the table in front of me.

"See, we think one of those men was actually killed in the warehouse and left there. The other three we believe were killed somewhere else then brought to the warehouse and . . . arranged so they'd look like they killed each other."

"But you were too smart for that, huh?"

"You bet we were," he said. "Three of them were shot, all with different guns, and one of them was hit with something—a crowbar, or something like that."

"Sounds like you do have a real odd one on your hands. Tell me about the phone tip you received."

He picked the photos up again and put them back in the envelope.

"Just that you—and they mentioned you by name, although they called you Eddie G—knew something about the dead men."

"And you took that to mean I killed them?" I asked. "Look, even if I do work for the Sands and the Sands is owned by the mob, I'm still just a pit boss."

"A pit boss who finds bodies and gets himself in trouble," Hargrove added, "or did you just have a bad few months last year?"

"I guess that depends on how you look at it."

He sat forward.

"Look, I know that you like keepin' your Rat Pack buddies out of trouble," he said. "If that's what's goin' on here—"

"What's goin' on here, Detective," I said, "is that you're holdin' me on the word of an anonymous caller who didn't even know my last name. And you're holdin' Jerry just because he was with me when you came for me. At the very least let him go. All he's guilty of is coming to Vegas for some gambling and relaxation."

Hargrove laughed shortly.

"Your friend the gunsel doesn't know the first thing about relaxation."

Suddenly, Hargrove stood up, turned, and walked out without another word.

An hour and twenty minutes later he came back in. He didn't close the door behind him.

"You're both free to go," he said. "You can find your own way back to the Sands, or home, or wherever you're goin'. Just remember this. If I find out you had anything to do with these killings I'm gonna come down on you so hard . . ."

I waited for him to finish the statement. When he didn't, I said, "I understand, Hargrove. I understand perfectly."

"Yeah," he said, "I bet you do." He opened the door. "Get out."

I got up and walked into the hall. He came out behind me and closed the door.

"Just down the hall," he said.

We walked to the next door, where he stopped and opened it.

"Out, gunsel," he said.

A few seconds later Jerry appeared in the doorway, glowering at Hargrove.

"I tol' you I don't like that word."

"Yeah, I know you did. Go on, get out of here, both of you."

Forty-one

THE POLICE STATION was on West Russell, just off Las Vegas Boulevard. We could have walked, but we were able to snag a cab easily for a ride to the Sands.

When we got back it was after 2 A.M. The cops had given us all the coffee we wanted, and we were coffee'd out. But for once I was as hungry as Jerry, so we went to the Garden Room and each ordered the $4.99 special.

"I thought they'd keep us there all night," Jerry said. "A few more hours and I woulda starved to death."

As I cut into my prime rib it seemed to me more like days than hours since we'd been in Tahoe with Sammy that morning.

Which reminded me.

"Shit, I'll have to call Jack early in the morning to arrange for the copter again. He's not gonna like why we missed it."

"It ain't your fault the cops hauled ya in," Jerry said.

"When this all started Jack told me not to find any more bodies, like last year."

Jerry shrugged.

"He don't know that we did."

"What did Hargrove tell you?" I asked.

Jerry gave me the rundown on his interrogation by the detective, and it was pretty much the same one I'd experienced, except that Hargrove had been much more aggressive with him.

"Cops always try that with me," he said. "They think they can break me down."

"Well, he kept me waiting longer than he questioned me. I assumed he was with you all that time."

"He left me alone for a long time, too." He shrugged. "It's just another cop trick. He didn't get nothin' outta me."

"Me, neither."

"I knew he wouldn't," Jerry said.

"How could you be so sure?"

"Easy," he said. "You had every chance last year—and tonight—to throw me to 'em, to keep yourself in the clear. You never did."

"I wouldn't do that to you, Jerry."

"I know. You're a stand-up guy, Mr. G."

We finished our meals and ordered some pie. Jerry had more coffee, but I stuck with water.

"Why don't we try to get to Reno tonight?" the big guy asked.

"I'd have to wake Jack, or Sammy, to arrange for the copter," I said. "The meet isn't until tomorrow night. We can get to Reno in the morning and have time to check it out."

"You know people in Reno, Mr. G.?"

"I know some people, and I can get around," I said. "I can arrange to get us a car."

"So all we gotta do now is get some shut-eye."

"Right," I said. "If I can sleep on a full stomach."

"Me, I sleep better on a full stomach."

"Why doesn't that surprise me?"

"You takin' care of the check, Mr. G.?"

"I got it, Jerry."

"Then I'm gonna go; I'm done in," he said. "Meet in the lobby again?"

"Yeah," I said, "make it nine-thirty, this time. Gives me time to call Jack early."

"G'night, Mr. G."

" 'night, Jerry."

He left the Garden Room and I signaled the waitress for the check.

I sat back. I was going to have to wake Jack Entratter early, unless he was in his office early again. He seemed to have a lot on his mind, lately, so it was real possible he would be.

I paid the check and headed for the elevators, but detoured to the front desk. Anthony was working, this time not alongside Caitlin.

"Where's Caitlin tonight, Anthony?" I asked.

"The weirdest thing happened," he said. "She quit."

"Oh? Why?"

"Beats me. I got the word when I came on. Now I got this guy to train."

There was another young man behind the desk, looking confused and lost.

"You're pretty new yourself, aren't you?"

"Yeah, but I catch on quick," he said. "Can't say the same for him."

"What about Caitlin?"

"She caught on quick," he said.

"She was real pretty," I said. "You, uh, have any luck?"

"Huh-uh, not me. She said she was into older guys."

"Is that a fact?"

"Yeah," he said, "in fact, she seemed pretty interested in you."

"How interested?"

"She asked a lot of questions."

"Too bad she's gone."

"Yeah." Anthony looked over at his shift partner. "No, Hector, not like that." He looked at me. "Gotta go, Mr. Gianelli."

"Sure," I said. "One more thing. Caitlin say anything about havin' a boyfriend?"

Anthony laughed. "Caitlin had lots of boyfriends but the same guy picked her up every morning."

"Really?"

"I gotta straighten Hector out, Mr. Gianelli," he said, apologetically.

"I tell you what, Anthony," I said. "You do that and I'll wait. This is kind of important."

Now it was Anthony's turn to look confused.

"Oh, well, okay," he said. "Let me just . . . I'll be right back."

"I'll wait here," I said.

He went over to straighten out the new guy. I leaned on the counter to wait for him. Hopefully, he'd be able to tell me something about Caitlin's boyfriend that would help me find him. Somebody was responsible for sending four guys to their deaths. Maybe it was two people who were running things. Maybe it was Caitlin and her boyfriend.

Forty-two

WE DROVE THROUGH the openwork metal arch that read RENO, THE BIGGEST LITTLE CITY IN THE WORLD. Originally, it had been erected in 1927 to commemorate a Highway Exposition that was celebrating the opening of the road over the Sierras, which, at the time, was a big deal. At first it had read RENO, NEVADA'S TRANSCONTINENTAL HIGHWAY EXPOSITION JUNE 25–AUGUST 11 1927. Three years later it was changed to the "biggest little city" sign, and had read so ever since. I'd heard word that they were going to update the sign and, by 1963, it would be neon.

"Is that true?" Jerry asked.

"What?"

"That Reno is the biggest little city in the world?"

"Not literally," I said. "It's just a slogan."

He nodded.

I was driving a rented Chevrolet Sedan that had been left at the airport for us by my buddy, Jim Rooker, who was a pit boss at the Reno Harrah's. It was easier than giving Jerry directions and, besides that, he was not thrilled about driving a Chevy.

Jim Rooker had also agreed to get us a room without either of our names on the register, but could only offer one with two beds. I said that was fine.

I drove down Virginia Street, Reno's main drag, past some of the other casinos—Circus Circus, the Primadonna, the Eldorado, the Nugget, the Horseshoe, and Harold's Club, the oldest casino in Reno.

People were walking up and down the streets, crossing from one side to another, going in and out of the casinos. People from all walks of life, all income brackets. There were men in suits, men in bell-bottoms and flowered shirts, women in dresses, jeans and short skirts.

Finally we came to Harrah's, one of only two casino/hotels in town. We parked and went inside, each carrying a small overnight bag. Sammy's fifty grand was in mine.

True to his word, Rooker had checked us in under his name and, by 11:30 A.M., we were in our room. The meeting was supposed to take place at 9 P.M.

"These people are pretty smart not to call on the phone," Jerry said, looking out the window.

"How so?"

"They don't give you a chance to argue over the money, or the place, or the time. They just send it in writing and you got no choice."

"We have a choice," I said. "We could not show up."

He turned and looked at me.

"That's a choice?"

"Not really," I said. "Not if we still want to help Sammy."

"What if Mr. Davis is still not tellin' us everythin'?" he asked.

"Hopefully, we'll find that out, in time."

Now he turned to face me head-on.

"So how do we find the meeting place?"

"Same way we got the car and this room," I said. "My buddy Jim Rooker."

"Ain't he gonna wanna know why?"

"He's not going to ask any questions," I said.

"Why not?"

"Because I know some stuff his wife doesn't know."

"Ah . . ." He nodded with a knowing look.

"Come on," I said. "Let's go and find Jim."

✳   ✳   ✳

Jim was in his pit and he agreed to meet us outside in half an hour. He wanted a cigarette and some fresh air.

Outside, on the street in front of the casino, I said, "Jim, this is Jerry."

They nodded at each other.

Jim was ten years younger than I was. I had trained him at the Sands and he ended up getting married, moving to Reno, and landing this job at Harrah's. I knew two things about him that he didn't like people to know. One, he was unfaithful to his wife, and two, he loved her. He could not reconcile the two things, except to tell me once that a "new piece of ass" was too much of a challenge to him.

"Walk with me, guys," he said, and we started down the street, me next to him, Jerry behind us.

"Here are your directions," he said, handing me a slip of paper. "That's in the middle of nowhere, you know. That area gets used for lots of, whatayacallit, clandestine meetings? Sex? Drugs? The whole shebang. But I guess that's why you've got Jerry with you."

We got to the end of the block and he stopped. Across the street, on the corner, were three streetwalkers in skimpy tops, short skirts and high heels. He waved and they waved back, laughing and calling out his name.

"How's Enid?" I asked.

"She's fine," he answered, still waving. "I told her I'd be seeing you and she sends her love."

I had introduced him and his wife while they were both working at the Sands.

"She also wanted to know if we could have dinner together, the three of us," he said. "I told her you would be in and out real quick and didn't have time."

"Is it me who doesn't have the time," I asked, "or you?"

"Does it matter?"

"No."

He checked his watch.

"I only took a ten-minute break. How's your room?"

"Fine."

"And the car?"

"Crap," Jerry said.

"It's no Caddy, but it was the best I could do on short notice."

"It'll do," I said.

He took a last drag on his cigarette and tossed it into the gutter.

"Is your friend gonna gamble while he's here?" he asked.

"No," I said. "We're not here to gamble. I'm just gonna show him some of the casinos."

"And drive out into the middle of nowhere," he said.

"Jim—"

"I know, none of my business. Stop by the pit and say good-bye before you leave."

"I don't know if that'll be tonight or tomorrow," I said.

"Whenever."

"Okay."

As Jim walked away Jerry said, "We better not find no bodies this time. He's gonna remember we went out there."

"I know," I said. "We'll just have to hope that this time we just make the buy."

Forty-three

W<small>E AIN'T HEARD NOTHIN'</small> from any of them people you talked to," he said. "The girl, the kid, uh, that car jockey—"

"They'd only call if they knew something," I pointed out.

We didn't go back into the casino right away, just stood there on the corner. The hookers called out to us but Jerry waved them away with a big hand.

"We should take a drive and check out the location," I said.

"You never told me what you found out about the girl, back in Vegas," Jerry said.

"She had a boyfriend who picked her up every day," I said. "Anthony said he was in his late twenties with dark hair."

"Big guy?"

"Average."

"Good-lookin'?" he asked. "He'd have to be good-lookin' ta get a dame like that."

"Maybe," I said. "Anthony didn't say."

"He know anything else, this Anthony?"

"No," I said, "nothing helpful."

"You'll never see her again," he said, "unless she's at the meet."

"How likely is that?" I said. "Her job was probably to get that note to me, and that's it."

"So they put her in the hotel just in case they had to use her?"

"Seems like it."

"That means they were prepared for somethin' ta go wrong."

"And it did. Jerry, would that mean they were pros?"

"Naw," he said, "this's all been way too messy for pros. Just means they been thinkin', plannin'."

"Well, their plan seems to have a lot of flaws in it. Let's hope this part of it goes right."

Jerry didn't look too convinced.

That made two of us.

Jerry read the directions while I drove. We left the Reno strip behind and drove out into the country. I wondered what it was that made the area so bad. It was a far cry from the warehouse where the first meet had been set.

Then we passed by homes badly in need of repair and I started to see what Jim had meant. This section was no doubt populated by people who kept rifles in their homes. I could feel them eyeing us with suspicion as we drove by.

Eventually, we reached a point where the street turned to gravel.

"Supposed to be at the end of this road," Jerry said. We soon left gravel for a dirt road.

As we reached the end of the road we came to a freestanding barn, with the burnt-out remnants of a small house standing—if you could use that word—next to it.

I stopped the car in front of the barn and we got out.

"Plenty of cover here," Jerry said, looking around. There was brush he could hide behind, as well as hills and dips.

"I'd have to drop you where the road begins," I said, looking behind us. "The rest of this ride is in plain sight."

"That's okay," he said. "I can hike it."

I looked at him. Jerry was a city guy, and this was rough terrain.

"Don't worry," he said, as if reading my mind, "I'm in shape for a hike."

"Let's go have a look," I suggested.

The inside of the barn was empty, and had obviously been empty for a long time. There were rusted tools and dried-out bales of hay strewn about.

"I've got an idea," Jerry said. "I'm gonna have a look at the house."

"You mean what's left of the house."

"I think there's enough."

"Enough for what?" I called after him, but he left the barn.

I walked around for a few more minutes. The back doors of the barn were falling off their hinges. There was no way anybody could possibly get locked in.

I walked over to the house. There were only two walls left, and they faced the barn. One wall still held the front door, and Jerry came walking through it.

"I can stay in here," he said.

I looked up at the sky.

"Unless there's a lot of moonlight you're gonna need a flashlight."

"Somebody'll see it."

"How will you find your way to that house in the dark?" I asked.

"No," he replied, "I'm sayin' now. I can stay here now so that I'm already here tonight."

"Jerry, that's hours away. And what happens if they get the same idea, to put a man in that house?"

"It won't be big enough for the both of us."

"I don't like it."

"It's a good idea."

"I didn't say it wasn't," I said. "I'm just sayin' I don't like it."

"Mr. G., it's the best way to go," he said. "If somebody gets the same idea I'll deal with it. But it's your call."

"I know it," I said. "Just give me a minute."

While he waited, Jerry walked completely around what was left of the small house.

"Jerry—"

"I'm good, Mr. G.," he said. "I got my forty-five, and I just ate."

I looked up at the sun, which was shining brightly.

"You have no water."

"I won't die," he said. "The sun'll go down soon."

"And then it'll get cold."

"Cold don't bother me."

He was wearing a sports jacket over a short-sleeve shirt.

"You don't know what cold is like in the desert," I warned him.

"Let's check the trunk of the car," he said. "Maybe there's a blanket."

We walked to the car. As we approached it, we saw clouds of dust in the distance.

"A car," he said, "comin' fast."

"I guess they got the same idea a few minutes after we did," I said. "Let's pull the car into the barn, just in case they haven't spotted us, yet."

"Let's push it," he suggested.

We put the Chevy in neutral and pushed it into the barn, then stayed in there with it while the car approached.

Jerry slid the .45 from his holster, and we waited—at least one of us with bated breath.

Forty-four

THE CAR PULLED to a stop outside the barn. The driver got out, then the back doors opened and two more men got out. They were all wearing suits and, since the dust had not yet settled, they started slapping at their jackets and pants.

"Feds," Jerry said.

I turned my head quickly. We were watching them from between slats of wood in the barn wall.

"How can you tell that?" I whispered.

"The car, the suits, the hats," he said, "an' the ties."

"Really?"

"They ain't the sellers," he said. "They're too well dressed. An' they ain't the mob on account of they ain't dressed good enough."

I couldn't argue with him. He had the experience edge on me.

I looked back outside. They were milling about, looking at the ground. One of them walked over to the half-a-house and took a look, then he turned and pointed at the barn. The other two nodded, and they all turned to face us.

"Come on, Mr. Gianelli," one of them said. "We can see by the tracks your car made that you're in the barn."

"What the fuck—" I said. "Who are these guys, Daniel Boone?"

"Feds," Jerry said again, and if possible he made it sound like an even dirtier word than when he said "Cops."

"And if you or your big friend have a gun, please toss it out first," a second man said. "We'd hate for any accidents to happen."

I turned and looked at Jerry.

"I guess we better do it."

"Yeah," he said, then added, "unless you wanna shoot it out?"

"Gee," I said, "I only wish I had a gun, then I would, but we're a little outgunned here, don't you think?"

"It was just a thought."

He tugged his .45 free from his shoulder holster, walked to the door and tossed it out.

"Gonna have ta clean the damn thing when I get it back," he muttered.

I walked to the door and shouted, "We're comin' out."

"Come ahead. Hands in the air!" came the reply.

Jerry and I raised our hands and walked out of the barn.

The three men were identically dressed and, except for slight differences in height and weight, alike in appearance, as well.

"Frisk 'em," one man said, and as the other two approached us the first took out an ID holder and flashed it.

"My name is Agent Sloane, these are Agents Simpson and Byer."

"Agents?" I asked. "FBI?"

"No, sir," Sloane said, "Secret Service."

"Secret Service?" I repeated as Byer did a quick pat-down on me and Simpson did the same to Jerry—although it may have been the other way around. I was glad I'd left the money in the hotel safe.

I looked Byer—or Simpson—in the eye and said to the three of them, "Can I see all your IDs up close?"

Sloane came closer, while Byer and Simpson—mine did turn out to be Byer—opened their ID holders. They all had credentials imprinted with UNITED STATES SECRET SERVICE on them.

"Can we put our hands down now?" I asked.

The three of them backed away a safe distance and Sloane said, "Sure. And while you're at it produce your own IDs."

We lowered our hands, took out our wallets and handed them over.

"Edward Gianelli?" Sloane asked, looking at me.

"That's right."

He gave Byer our wallets so he could hand them back to us.

"Who was carrying?" Sloane asked. Byer went over, retrieved the .45 and carried it to Sloane, who tucked it into his belt.

"I was," Jerry said.

"You got a permit?"

Jerry took it out and handed it to Byer, who carried it back to Sloane. There was absolutely no doubt who was in charge, here.

"This is for New York and New Jersey."

"That's right."

"I don't know if you're aware of it, Mr. Epstein, but you're in Nevada."

"I'm visiting."

"Why were you carrying?"

"For protection."

"Against what?"

"You didn't need my wallet to know who I was," I said, interrupting. "You called out to me by name."

Sloane looked at me, then handed the permit back to Byer, who gave it to Jerry. Apparently, the head man had decided to let Jerry off the hook for a while.

"You're right, Mr. Gianelli," Sloane said, "I do know who you are. What I'd like to know, however, is what you and your friend are doing here."

"What are *you* doing here, out in the middle of nowhere?" I asked.

"We heard there was a buy going down," he said, candidly. "So what are you doing, sir, buying or selling?"

"Damn, you guys are polite," Jerry said.

Sloane looked at Jerry.

"I'm sure you're used to dealing with New York and New Jersey cops, Mr. Epstein. We could've shot you in the kneecaps and we'd still be more polite than they are."

"You got that right."

"But don't think for a moment that means you can fuck with us."

"Wait a minute," I said. "Nobody's tryin' to fuck with you, but isn't your job safeguarding the President of the United States?"

"That's right."

I looked around and said, "I don't see JFK anywhere around here."

"The man doesn't have to be here himself for us to be investigating a danger to him."

"You think we are a danger to Jack Kennedy?"

Sloane's eyes narrowed.

"I'm sure the President wouldn't like you calling him Jack, Mr. Gianelli."

"Well, you might ask him that when you see him, Agent Sloane. It happens I know Jack Kennedy personally."

Jesus, but I was stretching the truth. I'd met Kennedy through Frank, and that was a year ago in Vegas. I wasn't even sure Kennedy would remember.

"Be that as it may," Sloane said, "I still need to know why you're out here."

We still had some hours before we were due to make our buy, but I didn't want to stay out there any longer than we had to.

"Do we have to do this here?" I asked. "I don't know what you came out here lookin' for, but you found us, and I'll bet we're not it."

None of the agents replied.

"It's hot out here," I said, "you guys are wearin' suits and we're wearin' sports jackets. Why don't we go back to town and do this where it's cool, and we can get something wet?"

"Suits me," Jerry said.

After a few seconds Agent Byers said, "Me, too," and then seemed to realize he'd said it out loud.

"Okay," Sloane said, "let's go get something wet."

Forty-five

I DID SOME CONVINCING that I was very proud of.

First, I convinced them that we had to bring our car. Sloane put us in the backseat of their sedan and Byers drove our rental.

Second, I convinced them that we had driven there directly from the airport, and had not checked into any hotel. It was the same with them.

Third, I convinced them that the bar in Harrah's would be the best place to talk and get a drink. They didn't know anything about Reno, so they went along with it.

"But don't try anything until we're finished talking," Sloane said.

I smiled from the backseat and said, "We've got no reason to try anything, Agent Sloane."

"Yes, well," Sloane said. "I guess you'll have to convince us of that."

We got a table in the back of the lounge and pulled some extra chairs over. We weren't exactly blending into the background, but that didn't seem to bother our Secret Service friends.

A pretty waitress showing lots of leg and cleavage came over.

"What can I get for you gentlemen?" she asked.

"Five cold beers," Sloane said.

"Any particular kind?"

"Just whatever you have on draft will do," he said.

"Comin' up."

"You mind if I ask the first question?" I said to Sloane.

"Yes."

"How did you know my name?"

"I said I minded."

"Oh, sorry," I said. "I thought you meant yes, I could ask the question."

"I understand you're a bit of a wise guy, Gianelli," he said. "That doesn't impress me."

I wasn't exactly sure which definition of "wise guy" he was referring to.

The waitress returned with five draft beers and leaned over, showing lots of skin while she set them down, attracting the eyes of the other two agents. But not Sloane.

"Anything else?" she asked.

"No," Sloane said, "can you just run a tab for us, honey?"

"Sure."

As she left the other two agents and Jerry lifted their glasses.

"I need to know what you and Mr. Epstein were doing out at that barn, Gianelli," Sloane said.

I picked up my beer meaning to sip it, but it was so good I ended up taking several long gulps before setting it down.

"You said you heard somebody was making a buy," I countered. "What kind of buy?"

"We're not going to get anywhere if we each keep asking questions and nobody answers," he said.

"Agreed."

We stared at each other and I wondered if he was going to pull rank.

"All right," he said. "You answer a question, and then I will."

Jerry and the other two agents were watching us, intrigued, waiting for the next move.

"Okay, we were out there scouting the area because *we* are supposed to have a meeting tonight to make a buy."

"And what are you buying?"

"Photographs," I said. "That is, negatives for a roll of photos."

"An entire roll?"

"Yes."

"Why?"

"There's at least one photo on that roll that somebody thinks is worth fifty thousand dollars."

"Fifty thousand?"

"That's right."

"You're going to pay somebody fifty thousand dollars for one photo?"

"The problem is, we don't know which one," I said. "That's why we need the whole roll."

"Where's your buy money?" Sloane asked.

"In a safe place."

Suddenly, I wanted to take another look at their IDs. I just had a bad feeling.

Byers and Simpson started to laugh.

"Fifty thousand . . ." Byers said, shaking his head.

"What's funny about that?" I asked.

"Mr. Gianelli," Sloane said, "you'll be interested to know we are also here to buy a photograph—only we're paying half a million bucks."

Forty-six

HALF A MILLION?" I asked, after picking my jaw up off the table.
To his credit Jerry didn't flinch.

"Not a lot of money, considering where we are, is it?" Sloane
asked.

"Half a million dollars is a lot of scratch no matter where you are,"
I said. "Are you thinkin' you're makin' your buy from the same people
we're makin' ours from?"

"How many rolls of film can there be?" he asked.

"Are you after the roll, or a particular photo?"

"One photo," he said, "but we'll buy the whole roll to get it."

"So why would these people want fifty thousand dollars from one
man when they're gettin' half a million from . . . who? The President?"

"Who's your principal, Gianelli?"

"I think that's a question I won't answer, Agent Sloane."

"Same here."

"So when was your meet set for?" I asked.

"We're staying at a small hotel just outside of town," he said.
"They'll contact us there."

"Well, our meet is set for tomorrow morning," I said.

"What were you doing out there today?"

"Scouting it," I said. "Jerry, here, is supposed to be my backup. We were lookin' for a place for him to set himself."

"I see."

"Are you going to let us make our buy?"

Byers and Simpson finished their beers and stared at Sloane.

"What time's your meet?"

"Ten A.M."

"When is Jerry going out there?"

"Seven."

"Maybe," Sloane said, "we should let Agent Byers go out with him."

"Is that the only way we get to complete our transaction?"

"Yes."

"Okay, fine," I said. "Jerry and Byers can meet out in front of Harrah's."

"Fine," Sloane said. "Then Agent Simpson and I will meet you at, say, nine? Same place?"

"Sure," I said. "Out front. Jerry and Byers can use our car, and we'll use yours."

Sloane drank half his beer and set it down. The three men stood up.

"We'll see you gents in the morning, then."

"Not going to do any gambling while you're here?" I asked.

"We'll do plenty tomorrow," Sloane said, "with our lives. What about you two? Where will you be spending the night?"

"Hey, this is Reno, baby," I said. "It's open all night. We'll be fine."

They started to leave and Jerry said, "Ain't you forgot somethin'?"

Sloane turned and looked at him.

"Like what?"

"My piece."

Sloane smiled.

"Oh, yeah."

He took it from his belt, passed it over, then headed for the door. Byers and Simpson waved and followed Sloane out of the lounge.

"They didn't ask enough questions," Jerry said.

"I know."

"I don't think they're Feds," Jerry said.

"Maybe not. That's why I told them our meet was tomorrow," I said.

"Why do you think they're here?"

"It sure isn't to pay anybody half a million dollars," I said. "I wouldn't trust them with that much money."

"What if the money man was comin' later?"

"What if they *are* from Washington," I said. "Not exactly Feds, but . . ."

"What are you sayin'?"

"I'm thinking out loud," I said, "and if I'm gonna keep on doin' it we need two more beers."

I waved to the waitress. When she had us set up I started to talk. I was trying it out on Jerry, and on myself, out loud.

"I'm thinkin' about the first dead guy in the warehouse, Jerry. What if he wasn't killed by one of his partners? What if somebody met him to make a buy and killed him instead?"

"These guys?"

"Why not?"

"And you think they're here to kill somebody else?" Jerry asked.

"If there's a picture that's worth a half a million bucks, then there'd be a picture worth killing for. I see two scenarios. One, these guys are lookin' for the picture for themselves."

"And two?"

"They were sent to make a buy, but what they really want to do is get the picture and kill everyone and anyone who saw it."

"From Washington?" Jerry said. "You mean you think JFK sent these guys out to kill instead of buy?"

"Maybe not Jack," I said, "maybe Bobby. He'd do anythin' to protect his brother."

"So Mr. Davis got a photo of JFK doin' somethin' he's not supposed to be doin', with somebody he ain't supposed to be doin' it with."

"You know, I actually followed that."

"So how do we find out?"

"Today we make some calls, and tonight we go to the meet. Maybe we can convince the seller of Sammy's picture to come clean by tellin' them all of this. We can't forget that our part in all this is to get Sammy his picture back."

"So who we callin'?"

"Somebody who can answer a few questions about the Kennedy clan."

"Mr. S.?"

"No," I said, "Peter Lawford."

"That guy?" Jerry made a face. "Why would he talk to you?"

"Because Sammy's gonna ask him to," I said, "and they're buddies."

"Wait a minute, Mr. G.," Jerry said. "What happens to us if we see that picture?"

"One thing at a time, Jerry," I said, "one thing at a time."

Forty-seven

WE WENT BACK to the room and I called Sammy in Tahoe.

"You're a cool cat, you know that, Eddie?" Sammy said when I was done. "You were lookin' to keep me out of the loop, weren't you?"

"For your own good, Sam."

"So what's changed, man?" Sammy asked. "Why the call now?"

"I've got a theory," I said.

"About my pictures?"

"Yup."

"Do I get to hear it?"

"Only because I need to talk to Peter, and you can get him to call me."

"Peter . . . Lawford?"

"Right."

"Listen, Eddie, Frank and Peter, they're—"

"This'll have nothin' to do with Frank, Sammy."

"But . . . you're sayin' this is about the President, aren't you? About Kennedy?"

"That's right, Sammy. I think you caught JFK, maybe in the background of a photo, but you caught him doin' somethin' they don't want anyone to know about."

"What?" Sammy asked. "Takin' a payoff? Or was it a girl?"

"I don't know, Sammy," I said, "but it looks like they're killin' to keep it quiet."

"Jesus . . . so now we've got two pictures to worry about?"

"I don't know about you," I said, "but my first concern is still your picture. But can you get Peter to call me? Talk to me about the Kennedy family?"

"I can get him to call you," he said, "but whether or not he'll talk to you, that's somethin' else."

"Let's start with the call, Sam, as soon as possible. I'm at Harrah's in Reno. Here's the number." I read it to him off the phone.

"Stay put," he said. "Let me see if I can get ahold of him."

I checked my watch.

"It's got to be in two hours, Sam," I said.

"I'll try, Eddie."

I hung up and looked at Jerry.

"Why two hours?" he asked. "We got more time than that."

"Not if we stick to the plan we've got to get you out there while it's still light."

"Oh yeah, the plan," Jerry said. "Me in that broken-down house."

"With your trusty forty-five," I said, "keepin' me alive."

"I can do that, Mr. G."

"I hope so, Jerry."

"But if I'm gonna do it," he said, sitting down on one of the beds, "I better take a little nap."

"Yeah," I said, suddenly realizing how tired I was, "me, too."

"Should we leave a wake-up call?"

"Naw," I said, reclining on the other bed with my shoes on, "Sammy's call will wake us up."

I woke up a while later. Jerry was sitting at the table. He had his gun in his hand and was cleaning it. He had the TV on.

I sat up and he turned the set off.

"Hey, Mr. G. Just wanted ta make sure this thing would work if we needed it."

"What time is it?"

"You was asleep for an hour and a half," he said. "I woke up about twenty minutes ago. I checked the news. Still no word on those bodies in Vegas."

"Good."

I rubbed my eyes. I felt like I had slept for ten minutes.

"I'm gonna call room service for some coffee," I said. "I know this is a silly question, but do you want something?"

"Yeah," he said, "I could use a burger and fries."

I looked at my watch.

"We're going to have to get out of here in half an hour."

"Then you better call now."

"Right."

I called down and asked them to put a rush on two burger platters with coffee.

"Mr. G.?" Jerry said, as I hung up.

"Yeah."

"I got another piece."

"Huh?"

"Another gun," he said, "in case you want it."

"Not . . . not Sammy's gun—"

"No, no," he said, "that's still hid around your house in pieces."

"If the cops show up with a search warrant are they gonna find it?" I asked.

"Naw," he said, then added, "I don't think."

Did I want to carry a gun? No. I might end up shooting some-body. Wasn't that why I had Jerry around? Well, no, not exactly, but still, if somebody had to be shot he was sure as hell gonna be better at it than I was.

"That's okay, Jerry," I said. "I don't want to carry a gun."

"Suit yerself."

He finished cleaning his .45 by the time the food showed up. We had ten minutes to eat. For some reason, it was the best burger and fries I'd had in a long time.

When we finished eating we put on our jackets. Jerry hadn't packed a heavy one, so I reminded him he was going to be out there for hours and it was going to get cold.

"You're right," he said. He put on a second shirt, then grabbed the pickle off my plate and the rest of my fries—just a few—wrapped them in a napkin and put them in his pocket.

"In case I get hungry."

The last thing he did was slide his .45 back into his shoulder rig.

"Well," I said, "now that you're completely outfitted, we better get going."

Forty-eight

PETER LAWFORD HADN'T CALLED, and Sammy hadn't, either. That worried me, but I had to get Jerry out to that meeting place.

It was on the outskirts of town, not that long a drive at all, but once we got there it felt like we were in the middle of nowhere.

Jerry did a quick check of the two buildings—or the building-and-a-half—and pronounced us all alone.

"You sure about this, Jerry?"

"Dead sure, Mr. G. It's the best way."

"And if they find you out here?"

"They may not be pros, but it probably won't surprise them that we're bein' careful."

"Okay," I said. "I'll be back about fifteen minutes before the meet."

"Bring a flashlight, Mr. G.," Jerry said.

"I'll get one from my buddy, Jim."

"Okay," Jerry said. "Drive careful."

"I'll see you later, Jerry," I said. "Watch your back."

"That ain't what I'm out here for, Mr. G.," he said. "I'm out here to watch your back."

"Yeah, well, do me a favor and watch 'em both, huh?"

"You got it."

I started up the car, turned it around, and headed back down the dirt road.

I was walking through Harrah's casino when I saw her. You couldn't miss her. The blond hair, pale skin, red mouth, all those curves—and the crowd she was drawing. It was Marilyn Monroe, all right, wearing a long-sleeved checkered shirt tucked into tight jeans. She was alone, trying to clear a path for herself to walk as people crowded in around her, trying to talk to her or touch her. I thought the look in her eyes was confused, or . . . kind of vacant. She also looked scared. I remembered what Frank said about the movie company having trouble with her being on time for her scenes in *The Misfits*.

But right now she was just trying to walk, and having a tough time of it. I could see she was on the verge of panic, so I did the only thing I could think of.

"Okay, okay, clear the way," I shouted, wading in with my arms waving like a windmill.

Everybody turned to look at me, wondering who the hell I was. They shrunk back from me, because I looked like a madman.

"Outta the way, outta the way!" I yelled.

Marilyn looked at me, too, as I reached her and put my arm around her. Good God, but she felt good, a beautiful, solid girl who really filled out her clothes.

"Wha— who are you?" she asked. I could feel her breath on my face.

"My name's Eddie," I said. "I'm a friend of Frank's. Come on!"

I pulled her along, still waving my free arm. People pulled back from my perceived authority, and I knew I had to get her out of there before she realized I was nobody.

"Are you staying here?" I asked her.

"Yes, but . . . I couldn't find the elevators."

"Stay close," I said, and felt one of her arms go around me.

I took her to the elevators as some of the crowd started to follow us.

". . . the hell is he . . ."

". . . he think he's doin'?"

I heard the words behind us as I pressed the button for the elevator. Luckily, the car was already on the ground floor, so the doors opened.

"In you go," I said, giving her a gentle push. "Got your room key?"

"Oh, yes, but . . ."

"What floor?"

"Four."

I leaned in and pressed four, then started to step out. She reached for me as the doors closed. Her hand caught the front of my shirt and she kissed me quickly on the cheek. I admit it, my head swam.

"Eddie . . . thanks, honey."

"Any time," I said, and she was gone.

As the doors closed I looked around the casino to see if Clark Gable or Montgomery Clift were anywhere. I wondered if they were staying in the hotel, too.

Once Marilyn was gone, people started gambling again and I continued on to the hotel lobby. Things were back to normal for everyone but me. I had Marilyn's kiss on my cheek, her scent in my nose and still had the feel of her weight against me.

Oh boy . . .

When I got to the room I called Sammy. While it rang I cleaned Marilyn's lipstick off my face with my handkerchief, folded it carefully, and put it in my pocket.

"I called but you weren't there," Sammy said.

"You must've tried after we left."

"Yeah, I was late," he said. "I was on the phone with Rod Serling. We met a while back and got pretty friendly. You know Serling?"

"Just what I see on *The Twilight Zone*," I said.

"I was all set to do an episode early last year," he explained, "about a white bigot who wakes up in the morning a black man. The censors wouldn't go for it and nixed the deal. I was feelin' pretty low and that was when Frank came to me with *Ocean's Eleven*."

"Sammy," I said, cutting him off before he could continue the story, "did you get to Peter?"

"Sorry, sorry, I did," he said. "I got a number for you to call."

I wrote it down.

"Can I call it right away?"

"Yeah, he'll be there. He doesn't want his wife or his in-laws to know he's talkin' to you, though."

"I can understand that."

"He'll be there—" He stopped, probably looking at his watch, or a clock, "—for about another hour."

"Okay," I said. "I'll call him and then get back to you."

"I'll be here."

I hung up and dialed the number. After two rings a man answered and said cautiously, "Hello?"

"Peter? This is Eddie Gianelli, from Vegas—"

"Yes, Mr. Gianelli, I know who you are," he said. "I recall our meeting once or twice last year."

"Right."

"Look, I am only talking to you because Sammy asked me to."

"I understand that."

"However, I advise you to choose your questions wisely."

"Wisely," I repeated. "Okay, how's this? Who's sending men out to Nevada to kill some people who have a photo to sell, JFK or Bobby?"

"Jesus, Eddie, what are you talking about?"

"I want to know if the Kennedy family has been approached to buy some potentially damaging photos? And, if instead of buying them, they decided to kill the fuckers. Who would okay something like that, Peter? Would it be Joe, the old man? Or Bobby, the attorney general? Or maybe it's just the President himself?"

There was nothing from the other end, and then Peter's British accent asked in a hushed whisper, "Eddie, how the fuck did you know about the photos?"

"I didn't really," I said. "I was guessing. You just told me, Peter."

"Yes, I did," he said, "and I could get in a lot of fucking trouble for telling you."

"Well, we'll just keep it between us, then. How's that? Us and Sammy, that is."

"And Frank."

"What about Frank?"

"Would you, uh, tell Frank I helped you?"

I'd been hearing some things about Frank and Peter falling out, remembered what Frank had said the night we all went to Dino's show, how we didn't need Peter.

"Is that what you want, Peter?" I asked. "You want me to put a good word in with Frank for you?"

"Ah . . . I would appreciate it, Eddie."

"Well then, let's see if you actually do tell me something helpful."

He hesitated, then asked, "What do you want to know?"

Forty-nine

ACCORDING TO PETER the entire Kennedy clan was in an uproar over the threat of some photos being leaked to the press.

"What photos?" I asked.

"I haven't seen them, Eddie," Peter said. "They don't confide in me like that."

"Well, has anybody seen the photos?"

"I—I think Bobby has," he said, "and Joseph."

"And you have no idea what the picture shows?"

"No."

"Is it a picture of Jack?"

"Well . . . it would have to be, for them to be as upset as they are."

"Okay, here's the big question," I said. "Does Jack know what's going on? That his father and brother are killin' people for that photo?"

"Eddie, Bobby's only trying to do—"

"Does Jack know?"

"I doubt it," Peter said. "They try to shield him from things like that."

"Unpleasant things, you mean?"

"Yes."

"That figures."

"Eddie, what's going on with Sammy?"

"Didn't he tell you?"

"No—well, yes. He said something about a photo, but . . ."

"Somebody's tryin' to sell him a photo for fifty grand."

"Fifty thousand dollars? But—but that's nothing compared to . . ."

"Compared to what?" I asked. "To what the Kennedys are being asked to pay?"

"It doesn't make sense," Peter said. "Why would anyone also try to sell to Sammy for fifty?"

"I don't know," I said, "but I've got some ideas. Peter, I don't suppose if I gave you names you'd recognize them as Secret Service agents?"

"I wouldn't know them from Adam, Eddie."

I was thinking I'd gotten all the help I could out of Peter Lawford.

"Okay, Peter, thanks for talking to me."

"Oh, uh, Eddie?" He sounded like he was desperate to catch me before I hung up.

"Yeah, Peter?"

"You, uh, will mention to Frank that I was of assistance to you?"

"Sure thing, Peter," I said. "I'll mention it to him, as soon as I see him."

"Ah, thank you," he said, "thank you."

"You're welcome."

"Oh, Eddie!"

"Yes?"

"A word of advice?"

"Sure."

"Watch your step," he said. "If Bobby, or the old man, have sent men out there you'd do well to stay out of their way."

"I kinda figured that out for myself, Peter," I said, "but thanks."

After the call with Peter I officially wanted out. Whether there were Secret Service people out there killing people, or they were just some sort of government assassins, I didn't want to have anything to do with them. But with Jerry sitting out in the desert in that burnt-out half-a-house, I was stuck.

Unless I could get out there and get us both away from there before the meet time.

Fifty

I GOT TO THE LOCATION half an hour before the meet. It was dark already, so I left the headlights on.

"Jerry?" I called, getting out of the car.

No answer.

"Don't fuck around, Jerry," I called. "I'm here, I'm alone, and we have to get out of here!"

If Jerry wasn't there I didn't know what I'd do. If somebody had been good enough to sneak up on him and grab him, what chance did I—

"What's up, Mr. G.?" Jerry asked, coming out of the remnants of the house. "I thought—"

"I changed my mind, Jerry," I said. "I'm not as interested in helping Sammy as I was before."

"Why not? What's changed?"

"I'll tell you in the car," I said. "Let's get out of here."

He started toward the car, then said, "I think it's too late." He pointed.

I turned and saw headlights in the distance.

"Damn it!"

I ran to the rental car and doused the lights. Jerry was still staring at the road.

"More than one car," he said.

"I think those cars are filled with men with murder in mind, Jerry. We've got to get going."

"Where?"

"This road keeps going," I said, although it was barely a dirt road. "I don't know where to, but it's better than going back."

"Maybe not," Jerry said, with a smile, "if you let me drive."

I tossed him the keys. It was a better alternative than driving out into the middle of the Nevada desert at night.

We got in the car and Jerry started driving, his foot pressed to the floor. The car began gathering speed, and the headlights of the other cars were getting closer.

"We playin' chicken?" I asked.

"That's what we're doin'."

The road was narrow, only room for one car at a time. We needed the drivers of both cars to play chicken with us . . . and lose. If even one of them had the guts for it we'd end up in a head-on collision, because I knew Jerry wouldn't give in.

We were leaving a thick cloud of dust behind us, which didn't matter. It couldn't be seen in the dark. Besides, it was all about headlights, now. We could see theirs, and they could see ours.

Jerry and I didn't talk. He gripped the wheel fiercely and I held on for dear life. He was right to drive. With me behind the wheel we eventually would have ended up in a ditch somewhere.

"Hang on," he finally said, as the approaching headlights loomed.

Somehow, he managed to get more speed out of our car, and suddenly the headlights ahead of us veered off, one pair to the left, the other to the right. One of them simply kept going out into the dark of the desert, but the other one hit something and flipped over. It tumbled end over end, but we didn't stay to see where it came to rest.

I did turn to look behind us as we sped away. The car that was upright sat still, headlights on, but I could hear a wheel spinning. They were stuck.

"Are they followin' us?" Jerry asked.

"No," I said, turning back around. "You can slow down before you kill us."

He slowed, but not by much.

"Wanna tell me what's goin' on?"

"I think that first guy we found in the warehouse was met and killed by somebody who was sent by the Kennedy family."

"And the men we killed in your house?"

"I don't know," I said. "Secret Service, CIA, or just hired muscle. Whichever, they were being directed by someone inside the administration."

"Jesus," Jerry said, "the President?"

"That's the funny part," I said. "I don't think the President knows what's goin' on."

We were back on the paved road to Reno when I told Jerry what Peter Lawford had told me.

"Somebody's freelancin'," he said when I was done.

"What do you mean?"

"I mean whoever was after Mr. Davis's fifty G's is not playin' the game accordin' to plan."

"So while they're trying to get big money from the Kennedy family," I said, "somebody else decided to make a quick fifty grand on the side?"

"And got killed for it."

"The guy in the warehouse," I said.

"I still think his own people killed him," Jerry said, "for pullin' this stunt."

"But I got another note after he was killed."

"So he's got friends," Jerry said. "That dame who came to your room, and her boyfriend."

"They might be dead, too."

"If I was makin' the big play," he said, "I'd kill anybody who was pissin' in my pot."

"So we've got blackmailers killin' blackmailers, and government hit men killin' people," I said. "All the more reason for us to just get out. I mean, look what just happened back there. If we'd gone there for a meet, we'd be dead."

"Mr. G.," he said, "if there are hitters in town—private or government—I might be able to find out."

"I'm lookin' to back out of this whole business, Jerry," I said. "I don't think I want you to make any calls. Let's wait and see what happens after I talk to Sammy."

We drove in silence until we saw the lights of Reno.

"You saved my ass again, Mr. G.," Jerry said. "Comin' out there for me. I ain't gonna forget it."

"That's okay, Jerry," I said. "I think we're about even."

Fifty-one

WE WERE WALKING through the casino in Harrah's when I said, "I saw Marilyn Monroe in here earlier tonight."

"Yer shittin' me."

"I shit you not."

"What was she doin' here?"

"She's shootin' a movie with Clark Gable," I said. "*The Misfits*."

"Wow. She look good?"

I thought of the handkerchief in my pocket with her lipstick on it.

"She looked great."

We went up to our room to collect what few things we'd brought with us, which included Jerry's back-up gun.

We packed up and he took out the .38 and showed it to me.

"Still don't want it?" he asked.

"Considerin' everything that's happening," I said, "I'll take it."

"You know how to use it?" he asked, handing it to me.

"I know."

I tucked the gun into my belt, where it felt foreign, but comforting.

We had finished packing our bags and were heading out the door when the phone rang.

We looked at each other. The reason we were getting out was

because people knew where we were. We weren't sure if Sloane and his two friends were in either of those cars, but it was a good bet.

"Gonna answer it?" Jerry asked.

"No," I said. "They might just be checkin' to see if we're here. Let's go!"

We left the room and hurried down the hall.

"Wait," Jerry said, at the elevators. "There must be another way off this floor and to the lobby."

"A freight elevator. If this place is anything like the Sands it'll be this way."

"What about a stairway?"

I looked on either side of the elevator and saw a door.

"That'd be it, but we'd come out right by the elevators. This way."

I led him back up the hallway, past our room, to where I hoped we'd find the freight elevator. We had to go through a door, but we found it.

"We take this to the first floor and then we duck out the back," I said.

The door opened and we got in. As the door closed Jerry eased his .45 from his shoulder holster.

"No harm bein' ready," he said.

I put my hand in my jacket pocket and closed it over the .38. I was very tense when the door opened, but relieved when there was no one there.

We came out into a hall. I got my bearings and said, "This way," moving away from the casino toward the back of the building. We found a door that took us out to the parking lot.

When we reached the car and got in—me behind the wheel—Jerry slid his .45 back into holster and said, "Where are we goin'?"

"Tahoe."

"Why not back to Vegas?"

"That's probably where they'd expect us to go."

"We gonna find the helicopter pilot—"

"Forget it," I said. "We'll drive. It's only forty or fifty miles."

"Can we check into a hotel then?" Jerry asked.

"No, we'll go to the Cal Neva. Frank left me a key for the cabin whenever I wanted."

"So what do we do when we get there?"

"I'm gonna talk to Sammy, tell him exactly what I think is goin' on, and why I want out."

"Mr. G."

"Yeah?"

"What happens if they won't let us out?" he asked.

"You're out, Jerry," I said. "We can get you back to Vegas and put you on a plane to New York."

"What about you?"

"I'll have to try to convince them that I haven't seen any incriminating photos of the President, and I don't want to."

"How're you gonna do that?"

"I'll have to go through Peter Lawford, I guess. I don't know if Frank can get to anybody in the administration."

"What if you can't get in touch?"

"I'll have to, somehow," I said. "Maybe Jack Entratter can help me."

"I can still make those phone calls, you know," he said. "Find out about the hitters?"

"Yeah, okay, do that when we get to Tahoe. You might come up with something I can use."

We drove in silence for a while. I was tired, but so keyed up that my eyes were wide open.

"Mr. G.?"

"Yeah?"

"What about Mr. Giancana?"

"What about him?"

"He might be able to help you."

"He'd never get to the Kennedys," I said. "Maybe before Jack was President, but not now."

"You never know if you don't ask."

I took a quick look at Jerry, then put my eyes back on the road.

"Why would he do that for me?" I asked.

"I think he liked you when he met you last year."

"Have you seen or talked to him since then?"

"No."

"I wouldn't even know how to get in touch with him."

"I got a number you could call."

I hesitated, almost asked him if he'd make the call for me, but instead I said, "I'll give it some thought."

"You need to get some help wherever ya can, Mr. G.," he said.

"I know that, Jerry," I said. "Okay, I'll give it a lot of thought."

Fifty-two

WE PHONED SAMMY and woke him up when we got to the Cal Neva and let ourselves into cabin four. He invited us up to his suite but I wanted to go a different way.

"Why don't you come over here?" I said. "I want to be able to talk without anyone knowin' where we are."

"Okay, man," he said, "your call. Since you have no room service can I bring anythin'?"

"Coffee."

"Unless you want something stronger?" he said.

"Coffee's fine," I said. "The way I'm feelin' if I have a drink it might knock me right out."

"Where's your partner?"

"He's here."

"I'll be right there."

I hung up and walked to the window. I could see a portion of the lake from there.

"This ain't what I expected when you said cabin," Jerry observed.

"I know," I said, "when I first came to see Frank I thought I'd find somethin' more rustic."

"Huh?"

"Somethin' more . . . earthy, plain. Nothin' this fancy."

"Oh, yeah . . . rustic."

"How about a hike while we're here?" I asked.

"I was willin' ta hike for you in Reno, Mr. G.," he said. "Let's don't push it, huh."

Sammy had a driver who had him at the cabin, with coffee, inside of half an hour. The driver carried the tray in—coffee and some donuts—while Sammy gave me and Jerry a big hug each. Jerry wasn't used to that kind of demonstrative behavior, but he put up with it.

Sammy poured three cups of coffee, handed us each one, then sat down on the sofa. The driver went outside and waited in the car.

"My eyes used to get like yours when I was tired," he said. "Now this one stays clear." He pointed to the glass eye and laughed.

I noticed that his good eye was as red as both of mine.

"You want out, Eddie?" he asked.

"Sammy, I need—"

"No hard feelings," he said. "I appreciate what you've done, especially when it came to the gun. You can walk away."

"I need to explain this to you."

He sat back on the sofa and said, "I'm all ears, pal."

I told him what I knew, what I suspected, and what I thought. He listened without interrupting.

"Whataya think?" I asked when I was done.

"I don't know, Eddie," he said. "Hit men? Maybe from the CIA? Or Joe Kennedy?"

"Or Bobby."

Sammy dry-washed his face with both hands, then sat forward and sipped some coffee.

"Are you sure you're not . . . overreacting?" he asked.

"I don't think so, Sam. You know that you took some photos when Jack Kennedy was around. We talked about this as a possibility."

"Well, yeah," he agreed, "but nothing anybody would kill for."

"That you know of."

"I've wracked my brain, Eddie," Sammy said. "If I caught JFK with his pants down, I don't know it."

"Maybe it wasn't so much his pants down as his hand out."

"A payoff?" Sammy asked. "Making one or paying one?"

"What about that million dollars Peter wanted to show us last year? Remember?" I asked. "Didn't he say the hotel owners wanted to donate it to JFK's campaign?"

"Yeah, but there's nothin' illegal about a campaign contribution."

"Well, if you can't figure it out, I sure can't," I said. "My only move now is to try and get out of this alive."

"There's still the photo *I'm* tryin' to buy back," he said.

"I'm thinkin' that might be a dead issue, Sammy. And I do mean dead."

"You mean you think whoever was tryin' to sell me the photo is dead?"

"My theory is, they went out on a limb, tried to make some extra money on the side, and got slapped down for it."

"But if I hear from them again . . ."

Yeah, what if he did hear from them again. What if Caitlin and her boyfriend were still after their fifty grand? Could I just walk out on him?

"If you get another note let me know," I said. "But if they call this time, because notes don't seem to be working, then you tell them to call me personally. Tell 'em that's the only way you'll do it."

"But what if that's not what they wanna do. What if they just release the photo—"

"They don't make any money that way, Sam," I said. "These are greedy people. They could sell it to a tabloid, but not for as much. They'll do whatever it takes to get that money. Just play hardball with them. Tell them I'm the go-between and they have to discuss the details with me. Tell 'em that's the only way you'll do it."

"And what phone number do I give them?" he asked. "You're not goin' home, are you?"

"No, I can't go home until I clear this up," I said. "They tried something there once, already. Gimme a minute to think."

I poured myself some coffee while I thought the situation over. Sammy just sat on the sofa and stared out the window at the sky.

"Okay," I said, "if they call just arrange a time for them to call here."

"How do I get in touch with you?"

"Same thing, I'll be here," I said. "Also, if you can't get me call Jerry." I didn't have to send Jerry back to New York just yet. The big guy looked at me and nodded his okay.

We stood up and Sammy walked me to the door.

"I hope you're wrong about all this, Eddie," Sammy said. "I mean, I hope this isn't some big conspiracy. . . ."

"This country was built on conspiracies, Sammy," I said.

"That may be, but I don't need 'em in my life. I got enough grief."

"I hear ya," I said, and he left.

"Jerry," I said, "after what happened in Reno why don't you go with Sammy? Watch out for him."

"For how long?"

"I have a feelin' they're gonna move fast on this," I said. "I'd just feel better if you were with him for a while. We don't know what those Feds from Reno—if they are Feds—will pull."

"What about you?" he asked.

"I'll be okay," I said. "I've got your other gun. Get goin'."

"Gotcha, Mr. G."

Fifty-three

THERE WAS A KNOCK at the door about ten minutes later. I opened it, thinking it was Jerry.

"What'd you forget—"

It wasn't Jerry. It was two men with guns.

"Eddie Gianelli?" one of the men asked.

"You know that already, or you wouldn't be here," I said, with a calm that surprised even me.

I said they had guns, I didn't say the weapons were in their hands. No, one had a gun on his belt, the other in a shoulder holster. They stood with their hands on their hips, so that the weapons were displayed.

"Are you Eddie Gianelli?" the older one asked. He had about ten years on his partner. He stood up straight, the younger one slouched. Sometimes I think that's the definition of experience.

"The man asked you a question," the young one said, "twice. Don't you think it would be polite to answer him?"

"You're probably right," I said. I looked at the older one. Forties, I thought, like me. "Yes, I'm Eddie Gianelli."

"The one they call 'Eddie G'?"

"Well, I don't know who 'they' are, but yes, that's a nickname of mine."

"Well, Eddie G," the older one said, "somebody wants to see you."

"Who?"

"A very important man."

"The President of the United States?"

"More important than him."

"Who's more important than the President?"

Neither one answered.

I tried to judge them by their clothes, the way Jerry had done earlier with the other three. These two had decent suits and shoes, and thin ties. I gave up after that.

"What do I call you?"

"Call him Number Two," the older man said, "and me Number One."

"Why are you Number One?" the younger one asked.

The older one looked at him.

"Because I'm not dumb enough to ask a question like that."

"He's right," I said to Number Two. "That was a dumb question."

He came out of his slouch and asked, "You callin' me dumb?"

I looked at Number One, who shrugged wearily.

"Are you comin'?" he asked.

"What's my alternative?"

"We bring you."

"How far are we goin'?" I asked.

"Not far."

"Am I comin' back?"

"No reason to think otherwise."

For some reason I believed him. These actually were messenger boys, not hit men.

"Well," I asked, "when do we go?"

"Now," Number One said, "but first . . . you wouldn't be carrying a gun, would you?"

There was no point in lying, since they'd probably search me no matter what I said.

"As a matter of fact." I raised my hands and indicated my right jacket pocket.

Number One stepped forward and fished the .38 out.

"I'd like to get that back when we're done."

"Don't see why not," he said, tucking the gun into his belt. "Shall we go?"

Fifty-four

THEY HAD A BLACK sedan parked in the lot. Number Two got behind the wheel, Number One in the shotgun seat next to him. I got in the back. I didn't have a car.

"When will we—" I started, but Number One cut me off.

"There's no point in asking questions," he told me. "All we know is that we were to come and get you and bring you back. We don't know why."

"But where—"

"Where will be apparent shortly," he said, turning to look at me. "It's not far, like I told you. Just sit back and relax. Somebody wants to talk to you. Nobody wants to hurt you."

If I took him at his word this would probably be one of the few times I would actually be able to sit back and relax for a while.

We drove out of Tahoe and past some of the ski lodges that were going up almost as fast as casinos. There were also some impressive homes out this way. We were most of the way around the beautiful lake, almost to the California border, when the car pulled into a long driveway that led up to a palatial house. Whoever I was being brought to see had money, or friends who had money.

"Nice little cottage," I said. I got no reply.

Number Two stopped the car in front of the house and we got out. I followed them up the stairs and inside.

"Leaving the door unlocked is not smart," I said, "even around here."

"We're expected," Number Two said.

Behind me I heard Number One lock the door.

They took me to a room that was lined with books—a library, or a den. Since all I have is a living room, I can never tell the difference.

"Wait here with him," Number Two said to Number One.

"Okay."

We waited in silence. He stared off into space while I walked around and looked at the books, a mixture of classic fiction, nonfiction, and law books. That's as far as I got before my host entered the room.

"You can go," he said to Number One.

"Yes, sir." He headed for the door, but stopped just short of leaving. "Want me to stay outside?"

"Just stay in the house," my host said. "I'll only need you to drive Mr. Gianelli home."

"Yes, sir."

Number One left and closed the door behind him.

My host was a man in his seventies, gray-haired, ramrod straight, wearing an unmistakably expensive suit and wire-rimmed glasses.

"Do you know who I am?" he asked.

"I think so," I said. "I've seen photos. You're Joseph Kennedy."

"Yes, that's correct."

Father of the President of the United States. In point of fact Joe Kennedy always wanted his oldest son, Joseph Kennedy Jr., to become President, but after he was killed in World War II he turned his ambitions to his second oldest son, John F. Kennedy. He planned strategies, did the fund-raising, and generally oversaw the entire campaign. It was believed by people in the know that Joe Kennedy was pulling the strings on both Jack and Bobby and that he insisted when Jack became President that he appoint Bobby as attorney general.

"Would you like a drink, sir?"

"No, thank you," I said. "I'd like to know why I was brought here."

"I'll have some Irish whiskey, if you don't mind."

He walked to a sideboard and poured two fingers into a tumbler.

"Please, have a seat," he said. "I must sit, myself. I don't often leave the compound anymore."

I knew from television and newspapers that the Kennedy residence in Hyannisport, Massachusetts was referred to as "the Kennedy Compound."

The room had two maroon leather armchairs and we each took one, so that we were facing each other.

"I had you brought here for a reason, Mr. Gianelli."

"I hope so."

Joe Kennedy's entire countenance was a stern one. I'd never heard anything about the man having a sense of humor. Now that I was seeing him for the first time the lack of it was very evident.

"I understand you have been engaged in the pursuit of a certain photo."

I quickly wondered how to play this. If Joseph Kennedy wanted me dead, I'd be dead, so I decided to play it straight.

"Actually," I said, "I'm trying to buy an entire roll of film."

"I see. Do you know what this roll of film contains?"

"Not a clue," I lied.

"Then why are you trying to purchase it?"

"I'm acting on someone else's behalf."

"And who would that be?"

"I'm not at liberty to say, at this time."

"I see," he said, again. "One of your Rat Pack cronies?" He said "Rat Pack" with intense dislike. I knew he hadn't liked Jack consorting with Frank, but they'd needed Frank to deliver the Teamsters. As soon as JFK got elected, Frank was out.

I decided not to be passive.

"I understand you're trying to buy a photo, too," I said.

Kennedy frowned, but said, "Well, yes . . ."

"Do you know what it is a photo of?"

"I'm afraid I do," he said. "Do you?"

"Nope."

He studied me, as if trying to decide if I was lying or not.

"I've checked you out, Mr. Gianelli," he said. "You work for Jack Entratter at the Sands hotel, and you consort with Frank Sinatra, Dean Martin . . . those types."

"Types?"

"Show business types."

"The types you wouldn't want your sons to consort with, you mean?"

"My sons choose their own friends."

"Sure they do."

"Never mind," he said. "My point is that I've checked you out and while you work for the Sands you don't seem to be . . . what's the word . . . connected."

"Connected to what?"

"Please, Mr. Gianelli," he said, "so far we haven't been playing games with each other."

"Except for that bit about your sons choosing their own friends."

"All right," he said. "We understand each other, then."

I nodded as if we did.

Fifty-five

MR. GIANELLI, it might surprise you to know that I think you have the best chance of buying these photos."

"Is that because people have been dying to get them?"

I didn't mean for that to come out as a pun, but it went over his head, anyway. I also noticed that my Brooklyn had taken a hike. Once again, I was adapting to the company I was keeping. This time, I didn't much like it.

"I have heard about that," he said.

"Mr. Kennedy, do you know a guy named Sloane? Claims to be with the Secret Service?"

"I don't believe I do."

"Byers, or Simpson?"

"No. Apparently, there are some other parties trying to get those photos."

"And how did these other parties find out about them?" I asked.

"I don't know, really," he said. "My only concern at the moment is that they don't succeed."

"Mr. Kennedy," I said, "so far I haven't seen the photo you're talking about. In fact I haven't even seen the photo I'm talking about."

"I believe you."

"Furthermore, I don't want to see them," I said. "In fact, I want out of this whole business."

"That's unfortunate."

"Why? Because you won't let me out?"

"I am certain I have no control over the decision you make, Mr. Gianelli," he said. "I'm sure you are your own man."

"Then why is it unfortunate?"

"Well, I'm not sure the other parties involved will let you out."

"I'm kind of worried about that, myself," I said. "I don't want to end up dead."

"Maybe the only way to avoid that is to get ahold of that roll of film."

"And turn it over to you?"

"Only the print I am concerned with," he said. "The rest of the roll is yours, to do with as you see fit. Sell it, turn it over to your principal, whatever."

"Sell it?" I said. "What the hell do you think I am? I'm no blackmailer."

"I apologize," he said. "That was thoughtless of me. Of course you're not a blackmailer. I understand you know my son, Jack."

"We met before he became President."

"Yes, I believe he mentioned it to me. Last year, wasn't it?"

"Yes."

"At about the time the photo was taken, in fact."

"I guess."

"Your likeness wouldn't be on that roll of film, would it, Mr. Gianelli?"

"It's possible," I said, "but I don't think I was doing anything . . . objectionable."

"How fortunate for you," he said. "My son was not as lucky."

It was the first time I heard some hint of emotion in his voice—disapproval. Was that an emotion?

"I have a proposal for you, sir," he said.

"Let's hear it."

"I'll pay you, employ you, to continue your negotiations for that roll of film."

"But the people I'm negotiating with are not the same—I mean, they're only looking for fifty thousand—"

"And you have it, don't you?"

"Well yes, but—"

"Then there are two groups looking to sell?"

"That's my point," I said, "and yours is asking for a lot more money."

"Yes," he said, "I wondered about that." He frowned while he was wondering.

"Mr. Kennedy," I said, "you really have no idea who's running around claiming to be members of the Secret Service? Killing people? Trying to kill me?"

"I truly don't, Mr. Gianelli," he said, "but you know Tahoe, Reno and Vegas better than my people do. You won't blunder about as much as they have been doing."

"Could any of your people have gone into business for themselves?"

His frown deepened.

"That's always possible."

"And the buy amount you're dealing with? Half a million?"

"Who told you that?"

"It doesn't matter," I said. "Is there somebody out there running around with that kind of money?"

"Not in cash," he said.

"Then how—"

"That's not important," he said. "I want you to make your fifty-thousand-dollar buy. That way we both get what we want."

"And my man is out fifty grand."

"I will cover the cost," he said. "And I'll pay you, besides."

"How much?"

"Name a price," he said. "Five thousand? Ten?"

"I don't know," I said. "I guess I'll have to figure out how much risking my life is worth."

"But you don't have to risk your life," he said. "Make the buy. Pay the fifty thousand."

"Oh, I'm not afraid of being killed by the sellers," I said. "It's the other buyers I'm worried about."

"I understood you had some . . . help? Some . . . what do you call it . . . backup?"

"That's not what I call it," I said. "That's not my lingo."

"Mine, either, I'm afraid."

"But you're right, I do have someone with me."

"I'll pay him, too, then."

"Really? That's interesting."

"As I said, name your price," he said, then added, "within reason."

"No blank checks, huh?" I asked.

"I don't think either of us deals with very many blank checks in our businesses."

"No, I'd say you're right."

"I'll need you to make a decision, Mr. Gianelli," he said. "I must be getting back to the compound."

I hesitated. I knew he thought that no one would, could, or should make a decision until he got back. He was a man used to being in charge.

"My son is going to do great things in the White House, Mr. Gianelli," he said. "That is, if he's permitted to."

"Oh shit," I said, "you just had to wave the flag in my face, didn't you?"

Fifty-six

I DIDN'T WANT TO SEEM money hungry, but I also didn't want Joe Kennedy to think I was a fool, or that I came cheap. If you undervalued yourself people would have no choice but to do the same.

So we hashed out prices—for me and for Jerry—before Numbers One and Two drove me back to Harrah's. They pulled up in front and stopped the car just barely long enough to give me back the .38 and let me out.

When I got to my room I immediately called Jerry. He said things were fine with Sammy, and he'd be going on stage in a little while. I told him what had happened and he said he'd be right over. I let him in as soon as he knocked.

"They were waiting for me and took me for a little ride."

Jerry's eyebrows went up. "And they brought you back?"

"Yes, after I had a very interesting conversation."

"With who?"

"Joseph Kennedy."

"Yer shittin' me! The President's father?"

"In the flesh."

"What did he want?"

"He wanted to make a deal," I said, and relayed both the conversation and the agreement we had come to.

"So it's up to you and me?" he asked.

"It's supposed to be up to you and me," I said. "We'll have to see about that."

"But you're gonna stay with it?"

I took out two cream-colored envelopes and passed one over to him.

"We're both stayin' with it."

Jerry opened the envelope, rifled through the bills, saw that they were all hundreds.

"How much is here?" he asked.

"Ten grand."

"For me?"

"And that one?" He indicated the envelope in my hand.

"Mine."

"The same amount?"

"Yes," I lied. No point telling him I'd only taken five thousand up front. "There'll be a bonus if we can deliver the goods."

"The goods being a picture of President Kennedy doin' somethin' illegal?"

"Doin' somethin' he shouldn't be doin'," I said, "but I can't say it's illegal. I can't even say what it is because I wasn't told."

"We'll know it when we see it."

"If we see it," I said, "and I'm still not sure I want to."

"I don't care what he's doin' in the picture," Jerry said. "I didn't even vote for 'im. So whatta we do? Buy it and not look at it?"

"If we can buy the entire roll of film, we'll be able to do just that."

"You're figurin' if we see the picture they'll kill us, too?"

"Somebody might try," I said, "but according to Joe Kennedy nobody workin' for him will try it. He gave his word."

Jerry laughed. "The word of a politician?"

"Yeah, I know. We can trust him about as far as we can throw him."

"Why are ya doin' it then, Mr. G.?"

I thought about the question. The money? The flag? To finish up a favor for Sammy?

"I kinda liked JFK when I met him last year," I said, finally. "I got the feeling running for President wasn't somethin' he wanted to do. I think he's lettin' his father run his life—or ruin it."

"Ruin it? How can bein' President of the United States ruin your life?"

"I got the feelin' when Kennedy was here last year he had interests other than . . . politics."

"Like broads?"

"Like havin' a good time," I said. "That can mean women, it can mean a lot of things. But when Joe Kennedy lost his oldest son, Jack's wants and needs suddenly came second. Now Jack is President and he's got all the headaches that come with it. I figure the last thing he needs is some photo showin' up in the papers givin' him more."

Jerry studied me for a few moments, then tucked the envelope full of money into his inside jacket pocket.

"I like the way you put all that, Mr. G.," he told me, "so I'm in, too."

Fifty-seven

WE HAD BREAKFAST PLANNED with Sammy at a corner table in Harrah's coffee shop but he was late. I was about to call his room when he appeared. There was a smattering of applause as the other diners recognized him. He graciously waved and shook hands but otherwise no one approached him as he walked to our table.

"Sorry I'm late, guys," he said, seating himself, "but I got a call." He leaned forward. "You know? A call."

"I get it, Sam," I said. "What'd they say?"

"They asked if I still wanted the photo."

"And?"

"I said I wanted the whole roll of film like we agreed. They said okay, but the price is now seventy-five thousand."

"Did you tell them what we discussed?" I asked.

"Yeah, I told them they'd have to call you because you're the go-between. She went crazy—"

"She?" I said. "The caller was a woman?"

"Yeah. I didn't mention that?"

"No, you didn't," I said. "Try not to leave anything else out."

The waitress came over and we ordered breakfast—omelet platters for the three of us.

"Okay," Sammy said, "the phone rang this morning and I

answered. I thought it might be you but it was a woman—a girl, actually."

"What kind of voice?"

"Young, pretty . . . flirty."

"Sounds like a lot of broads," Jerry said.

Sounds like Caitlin, I thought.

"Go ahead, Sam."

"After she cursed at me for a few minutes I got some backbone and told her that if she didn't contact you, there would be no deal."

"Nobody said you didn't have any backbone, Sammy."

"I said it," Sammy said, then pointed at both of us and with a crooked smile added, "but I'm the only one who can."

"Agreed," I said.

He looked at Jerry.

"Hey," the big man said, "you scare me."

"Yeah, right," Sammy said. "I'm about as big around as your leg."

"Can we get back to business?" I asked. "What did the girl say?"

"She cursed some more, but then she agreed," he said. "She's gonna call you at noon today."

"Noon," I said. "We've got a lot of time to have a leisurely breakfast."

"And while we do," Sammy said, "you can tell me what you guys have been up to."

"Me, I been in my room," Jerry said, looking at me.

"Let's get some coffee," I said, "and I'll tell you a story. . . ."

The story went on throughout breakfast, and we were still eating by the time I was done.

"Man, that's freaky," Sammy said. "So I did catch JFK on film."

"Doin' somethin' naughty," Jerry added.

Sammy looked at him.

"You sound happy."

"I didn't vote for 'im."

I left out the part about Joe Kennedy basically hiring Jerry and me to stay at it, but Sammy was no dope.

"I hope you're gettin' some scratch outta Joe Kennedy for this."

"He's payin'," I said, "and he's willin' to put up the money for your buy."

"Works for me," Sammy said. "But you guys still have a problem, don't you?"

"Namely?"

"If Kennedy is tellin' the truth and his men haven't been tryin' to kill you, who is? And who killed the man in the warehouse?"

"I think we'll find it all out when we get the film, Sammy."

Before I was ushered from Joe Kennedy's presence he pressed a business card into my hand. I now had a way of calling him, which, he said, not many people had.

"Let's finish eating and go to my cabin," I said to Sammy.

"We've still got some time."

"I want to place a call and get that seventy-five grand. We're gonna need it, because we are definitely makin' this buy."

Fifty-eight

We ALL WENT BACK to the cabin and I called the number Joseph Kennedy had given me. I didn't get him, but instead talked to some minion who said the money would be hand delivered to me within the hour.

"Seventy-five G's?" Jerry asked. "Hand delivered?"

"That's what he said."

"You got the power, Mr. G."

"Not me."

"You made the call," he pointed out. "That's all it took to get seventy-five grand delivered to the door. I don't know about your world, but in mine that's power."

"The man's got a point," Sammy said. "I'm impressed."

"Well," I said, "let's see if the money shows up."

A messenger—a real messenger, with a uniform that said so—delivered an eight-by-ten envelope to the door within the hour, and before my noon phone call was supposed to come in.

I opened the envelope and there were eight banded stacks of bills in there, ten thousand a stack except for the one that had five.

"See?" Jerry said to me. "Power."

"By the way," I said to Sammy, "I've got your money here, in the other room." Taking five stacks out of the envelope I added, "You might as well take it now."

"Hey," he said, taking the money from me, "you don't have to offer me fifty thousand dollars twice."

"Especially since it's already your money."

Sammy was standing there, fifty thousand in his hands, when the phone rang.

"I'll get it," I said.

They watched me walk to the phone and lift the receiver.

"Hello?"

"Are you the go-between?" she asked.

"Hello, Caitlin."

There was a pause, then, "How did you—what the—"

"I missed you the other morning, you left in such a hurry," I said. "Of course, you did leave me a note."

There was a long period of silence during which I became sure she had hung up, or pulled her phone out of the wall, but then a sexy chuckle tickled my ear.

"Eddie G," she said, "you're so smart."

Behind her I heard a man start to speak, but she shushed him hard enough to make me deaf.

"Sounds like your boyfriend's upset."

"He'll get over it," she said. "You got our money?"

"I've got it," I said.

"Seventy-five thousand?" Her voice got husky.

"Every penny," I said, "but we've got to make sure of somethin', Caitlin."

"What's that?"

"We've got to stay alive long enough to make the exchange."

"Don't worry about that," she said.

"Oh, but I am worried," I said, "more about you than myself."

"That's sweet."

"If I'm readin' the situation right, you've already lost one of your partners."

She fell silent again.

"And I'm havin' my own problems," I added. "This is no big se-cret we have goin' here, you know."

She covered the phone and had an exchange with her boyfriend.

"There are too many people with guns runnin' around, Caitlin," I said. "This meeting place has to be a good one."

"Agreed," she finally said. "Do you remember where we met?"

Did I remember? We met at the Sands, in the lobby, where she was working behind the desk.

"Yes."

"Meet me out where all the cars are."

The parking lot?

"When?"

"Do you remember what time it was when you kissed me for the first time?"

Her code was a very personal one. Anyone listening wouldn't be able to figure it out. This was probably overkill, but I continued to go along with it.

She came to my room to wake me up for my 6 A.M. wake-up call. So I must have kissed her at about six-oh-five.

"I remember."

"Twelve hours later, plus four."

It would be good and dark by 10 P.M. in the Sands parking lot. If you stayed away from the lights you could find some black corners to meet in.

"Okay," I replied, "but when?"

I could hear her mind working, trying to come up with a way to tell me the day without actually saying it on the phone, but she was out of codes.

"Tomorrow night," she said. "Don't be late."

"Don't get killed," I said, and she clicked off without comment.

"What was all that about?" Sammy asked.

I explained Caitlin's attempt at communicating by code.

"So when are we meetin'?" Jerry asked.

"Tomorrow night at ten in the parking lot behind the Sands."

"That's pretty public."

"There are some dark corners back there," I said. "She only worked there for about a week, but she knows that."

"And are we really gonna give her the money?"

"That'll get us the roll of film—or prints of the roll—but it won't guarantee we'll get all the prints of the Kennedy picture."

"Or mine," Sammy said. "I mean, if this girl and her boyfriend are actin' on their own and there are still others involved, there could be plenty of prints out there."

"I guess there's always that chance when you pay blackmail money," I said.

"There's only one way to make sure a blackmailer don't come back," Jerry said.

Sammy and I looked at him. We both knew what he meant by that.

"But you've got to make sure you get *all* the blackmailers," I countered. "How do you do that?"

"You convince one of 'em to finger the others," he said.

We all knew there was only one way to do that, too.

The phone rang at that moment. We all turned and stared.

"Answer it," I said to Jerry.

"Maybe they're gonna change the meet," Jerry said, as he picked up the receiver.

"Hello? Yes. Hold on." Jerry held the phone out to me. "It's for you. Jack Entratter."

Fifty-nine

"HELLO, JACK."

"Don't hello me, Eddie. Where have you been?"

"Tryin' to stay alive."

"Is that supposed to be dramatic?"

"It's supposed to be truthful, Jack."

He hesitated a moment, then—in a tone not quite so aggressive—said, "Well, the cops were here lookin' for you. Your old friend Detective Hargrove."

"I'm not surprised."

"Seems he thinks you had somethin' to do with killin' four men."

"Did he say that?"

"No," Entratter said, "he insinuated it. But he was in your house and he said somethin' about how clean your living room carpet was. In fact, he said it was still wet. Why's he interested in your wet shag carpet?"

"Did he mention a bullet hole in the wall?"

"No."

"Probably keepin' that to himself."

"There's a bullet hole in your wall?"

"I told you, Jack," I said, "I'm tryin' to stay alive."

"You got the big guy with you?"

"Yeah. Jerry's here."

"Hargrove was askin' about him, too."

"He's okay."

"How much longer is this gonna take you, Eddie?" he asked.

"Not sure, Jack."

"Damnit—"

"I'm gonna wrap it up as quick as I can."

He sighed heavily into the phone and said, "Okay, kid, but do me a favor, huh? Check in."

"Sure, Jack. What are you gonna tell Hargrove?"

"Don't worry," he said. "I'll string him along. Just be aware that he's lookin' for you. If you're in Vegas, keep your head low."

"Gotcha, Jack. Thanks."

"Call me if you get in a real bind, Eddie."

"You know it, Jack."

He knew from experience that whatever happened I'd try to keep him out of it. But his offer was sincere.

I hung up and turned to face Sammy and Jerry.

"Cops?" Jerry asked.

"I guess Hargrove got his search warrant and went into my house."

"There's nothing there for him to find," Jerry said.

"Except for a wet carpet."

"So when did it become a crime to clean yer house?" Jerry asked.

"The cops are lookin' for you?" Sammy asked.

"Both of us," I said.

"He ain't gonna come here," Jerry said.

"Yeah, but we've got to go back to Vegas for the meet," I said. "We'll have to time it right."

"I'll call for the copter, have it stand by tomorrow," Sammy said.

"Tell the pilot it'll be tomorrow night, but he better be ready at a moment's notice," I said.

"Will do."

"Meanwhile, we don't have much to do but wait," I said.

"Anybody got a deck of cards?" Jerry asked.

"We're in a casino town," Sammy said, as he picked up the phone. "I'm sure we can get as many as we want."

"You want to play gin?" I asked Jerry. "Or poker?"

"Nope," he said. "I thought maybe you could teach me how to play blackjack."

Jerry was a quick learner.

"I've never seen anybody catch on to strategy as fast as this guy," Sammy said.

He was watching while I taught Jerry the rudiments of the game, and then played hands with him. Before long he was standing when he should, hitting when he should, and splitting when he should. He did everything by the book, never used instinct or a hunch.

"This game is easy," he said after he'd won another hand.

"It'll be different when you're facing a house dealer," I said.

"Is this the game you used to play when you first started goin' to Vegas?" Jerry asked.

"Yes."

"And how did you do?"

"I used to be a CPA. My math is good, so I did okay. But there are times when you have to toss out accepted strategies."

"Like when?"

"Like when you start losing with twenty to the dealer's twenty-one again and again," Sammy said. "That's when the game gets too frustrating to play. I've seen it make grown men cry."

"I watched them play at the Sands," Jerry said. "I never saw nobody cry. I seen 'em curse, and get mad, but I never seen 'em cry."

"You start playin' this game in the casinos," I said, "and I guarantee you'll see a lot of stuff you've never seen before."

"I ain't gonna play it in the casino," he said. "I only risk my money on the horses."

"Then why'd you want to learn how to play?" Sammy asked.

Jerry looked at Sammy and said, "Just a way to pass the time."

"Well," Sammy said, looking at his watch, "there's still time to kill."

Jerry smiled then and asked, "Room service, anybody?"

Sixty

JERRY AND I FLEW into Vegas about 8 P.M. the next night. We killed the day in Tahoe watching Sammy rehearse, checking out the Harrah's operation, playing some more blackjack in our rooms. Finally I called the pilot and he flew us in.

We were in the Sands parking lot at nine, with an hour to go before the meet. We decided to sit in my car and wait.

"Nothing should go wrong this time," I said. "Nobody should know about this meet, even if somebody was listening to our phone conversation."

"Unless the dame and her boyfriend blab to somebody," Jerry pointed out. "Ya know, if they got, like, one more partner they could still fuck it up and get us all killed."

When he said that I touched the .38. It felt heavy in my jacket pocket. Jerry had cleaned his .45 yet again the night before.

I was nervous, sweating as if it was ten degrees hotter than it was, but Jerry was cool and calm.

"Mr. G., you really gonna give this broad all that money?"

"I'm gonna give her some of it, Jerry," I said, "and use the rest as bait."

"Bait?"

"Joe Kennedy wants to know who's got that photo of JFK," I said.

"You wanna go after those guys?" Jerry asked. "They're not gonna be like yer girl and her boyfriend, ya know."

"I know," I said. "I don't want to go after them, but Joe Kennedy might. We may not know how many prints of these photos have been made, but like you said, there's only one way to make sure they don't get released to the public."

"So even though Kennedy ain't sent any of his own hitters out yet—or so he says—you think he will once you get him the names?"

"That's all he wants."

"You comfortable with that, Mr. G.?"

"I've given it some thought and, yeah, I am," I said. "I think they killed the guy in the warehouse and I think they'd kill Caitlin and her boyfriend if they had the chance."

"So you think she'll give them up to you?"

"If I can convince her that they'll kill her if she doesn't, yeah," I said. "Also, I'm holdin' back fifty thousand."

"What if she doesn't know who they are."

"There can't be two different factions holding those photos," I said. "Too much coincidence. It's more likely somebody in the original group decided to go out on their own."

"Caitlin and her guy?"

I nodded.

"You got any suggestions about where I should stand?" he asked, craning his neck to look around.

"I think you should stay here, keep your eye on me," I said. "About ten to nine I'm gonna start walkin' around. I figure she's gonna pick out one of these dark corners out here and draw me in."

"Naw," he said, "I gotta get outta the car, in case her boyfriend's around. I can't leave ya out there with your ass swingin' in the wind, Mr. G."

"I appreciate that, Jerry," I said, "but you're gonna have to stay low."

"I may be a big guy, Mr. G.," he said, "but I can stay low."

"Okay," I said. "Okay."

✳   ✳   ✳

When the time came Jerry said, "Let me get out first."

"Go ahead."

He opened his car door, closed it as quietly as he could, then drew his .45 before he slunk away between the cars. He was right, he was able to keep low enough not to be seen.

I waited a minute or two then opened the door and stepped out. I didn't close it as lightly as Jerry had.

I walked out in the center of the brightest light in the lot. I had to be as easy to spot as Jerry was difficult.

Time went by—seconds, then minutes. I checked my watch several times. Finally, it was ten-seventeen when I heard someone hiss at me from the darkness.

"Caitlin?"

"Over here," she whispered, and stepped out of the shadows.

I touched the gun in my pocket, but left it there. Likewise the envelope of money in my pocket. I had split the money into one third, and two thirds.

I walked over to the lamppost and she stepped out into the light.

"Give me the money," she said. She looked bedraggled: limp hair, pale complexion. Her eyes were wide with fear. "Quickly."

"Where are the photos?"

"You'll get the damn photos," she said. "I want the money first. Now!"

"Not until I see the photos," I said. "And the negatives. Or the roll."

"There's no roll," she said, impatiently. "The photos were developed."

"Where are the negatives?"

"We only have one," she said. "The one photo you're lookin' for."

She took a small white envelope from her pocket.

"Seventy-five thousand," she said, her tone filled with awe. "For one picture."

Sixty-one

I TOOK THE ENVELOPE from my pocket. We approached each other and exchanged envelopes. Hastily, she tore hers open and counted.

"You're way short!" she said, angrily. We had split the money into two envelopes. Jerry was carrying one of them.

I took the photo from the envelope she had given me and reluctantly looked at it, then checked for the negative, holding it up to the light above us to make sure it was the right one. It was. I could see how Sammy would be embarrassed by it.

"You cheater!" she snapped. "Tony, Tony!" she shouted and looked about wildly.

Suddenly, a man came into view, but he wasn't moving on his own, he was being pushed from behind.

"He cheated us—" she started, but then she saw Jerry behind her boyfriend. "What—"

"He jumped me," Tony said. "I didn't have a chance."

No, he didn't. He was barely out of his teens. Jerry towered above him and was more than twice his weight.

"You have a gun!" she shouted at him.

"He *had* a gun," Jerry said, and held it up for her to see. It looked old and rusted. "If he'd tried to pull the trigger this thing would have exploded in his hand."

"I didn't do nothin'," the boy said. "It was all her idea—"

"Shut up!" Jerry said, slapping the back of his head.

I reached out and snatched the money from Caitlin's hand.

"Hey!"

"Plans have changed, Caitlin," I said. "This is your partner? This kid?"

She dummied up.

"I can make her talk, Mr. G.," Jerry said.

She looked at Jerry and her eyes got wide.

"She'll talk, Jerry," I said. "Let's go inside, where we can be more comfortable."

We took them into the Sands to the security office, where Larry Bigbee, the second in command, gave us a room so we could talk in private—rooms where they usually took cheaters for questioning. There were no two-way mirrors, though. This wasn't the police department.

Jerry pulled me aside before we started. "Mr. G., I been grilled enough time by cops to know we should probably split them up."

"We will," I said. "Let's just get her to say a little bit first. It'll prime the boy."

We went inside. I put the two envelopes of money on the table, with the greenbacks kind of spilling out. They both sat with their eyes glued to the cash.

"Caitlin, come on, why would a smart girl like you hook up with a loser like this kid."

"Hey—" the kid said, but Jerry smacked the back of his head again.

"I had to have another partner," Caitlin said. "Ernie, my boyfriend—it was his idea, and they killed him."

"The guy in the warehouse," I said.

"He went there to trade with you," she said, "but they got to him first."

"Who's they?"

She pointed at Tony.

"His brother and his boys," she said.

"His brother?"

"Walter. The whole thing with the pictures was his idea."

"Which picture?"

"The one Walter thought was worth half a mil," she said.

"Have you ever seen that picture?"

"No," she said. "Walter won't show it to anybody."

"So he's the only one who knows what's on it?"

"Yeah."

"But your boyfriend Ernie, he recognized this photo?" I touched the photo in my pocket. "And decided to make some money on the side?"

"The half a mil was gonna be cut up," she said, "and we were only in for a small piece. So yeah, we figured we'd get some money from that Sammy Davis guy."

"So Ernie set the meet-up with me, but Walter got to him first and killed him."

"Yeah."

"So you took over."

"We were just tryin' to make some extra money," she said. "That's all. They didn't have to kill him."

"Where did you get this one?" Jerry asked. He grabbed the boy by the scruff of the neck and shook him hard enough to rattle his teeth.

"He was always hangin' around the gang," she said. "His brother let him hang around, but not do anythin'. And he had eyes for me right from the start."

"His brother," I said. "How did he get ahold of the film in the first place?"

"I don't know," she said, jerking her thumb at Tony. "You'll have to ask him."

I looked at Jerry. Almost time to split them up.

"Gimme my money!" she said, suddenly making a grab for it.

"I'll give you this envelope, and this envelope only," I said, holding it up. "Twenty-five thousand dollars."

"That ain't fair—" the boy, Tony, started, but Jerry smacked him.

The girl shouted, "Shut up!" She looked at me. "What do I have to do for it?"

"Tell me where to find the others."

"That's easy," she said, pointing at Tony. "He knows where they are."

I looked at Tony, who suddenly realized he had something to sell.

"That's right," he said, "I know where they are. But I ain't tellin' . . . unless you give me the money, not her."

"How about I just break your neck?" Jerry asked.

"No!" Caitlin said. "That's not fair."

She meant giving him the money, not breaking his neck.

But the decision was mine.

Sixty-two

I PULLED JERRY ASIDE.

"The kid's the one who knows where his brother and the others are, so why don't you take the girl outside."

"Gotcha," he said. "She ain't no good to us if she don't know where nobody is."

We went back to the table. Jerry grabbed Caitlin by the arm and said, "Up. Yer comin' with me."

"Where?"

"Never mind." He pulled her to her feet and propelled her toward the door.

"Eddie—" she said, but I kept my back to her as Jerry opened the door and shoved her out.

"What's goin' on?" Tony demanded.

"You have a chance to make a lot of money, Tony," I said, "and it's up to you if you want to share it with Caitlin or not."

Tony suddenly grinned and said, "She's a hot piece of tail."

"Yes, she is," I said, speaking from experience. "It'll take a lotta cash to keep her hot, too."

"What do I gotta do?" he asked.

"You know damn well," I said.

He nodded.

"Take out your wallet."

He hauled a cracked leather wallet from his back pocket and dropped it on the table. I went through it until I found his driver's license, which identified him as Anthony Peaks.

"Your brother have the same last name?"

"Of course."

"Same address?"

"No," he said. "We don't live together."

"So this whole scheme to sell these photos was your brother's big idea?"

"Yeah, that's right."

"How did he get ahold of them?"

"Search me," he said, with a shrug. "All I know is he got 'em. He said some big shot was gonna pay a lot of money for 'em."

"So when did you and Caitlin and her boyfriend decide to get in touch with Sammy Davis Jr.?"

"That was Ernie's idea, like she said," Tony answered, "but it was Caitlin who recognized the picture. She reads a lot of those Hollywood magazines. She saw what was in one of the pictures and Walter knew that the nigger would pay big money for it."

I slapped him on the back of the head, hoping he was still sore there from Jerry's blow.

"Hey!"

"Watch your mouth!"

"What'd I say?"

"Sammy Davis is a friend of mine," I said. "Watch what you say."

He looked totally puzzled.

I realized he had no idea that what he'd said might be out of line.

"Your brother let you in on which big shot was gonna pay?"

"Naw, but it must be somebody big if he wasn't worried about this ni—uh, the Sammy Davis picture."

If Tony had no inkling that the President was involved, I wasn't going to tell him.

"So your brother has all the other prints?" I asked.

"Yeah."

"Does he know this one is missing?"

"He took it back from Ernie when he killed him," Tony said, "but Caitlin had made a copy."

"Okay, Tony, here's the big question," I said. "Where do I find your brother?"

"Him and the others . . ." he started, but then he trailed off.

"How many others?"

"He's got two buddies, Denny and Paul."

"And they killed Ernie and the others in that warehouse?" I threw in the others because we weren't supposed to know who killed them.

"Naw, we don't know who those other guys were or how they got there."

"I want those photos, Tony, and the negatives."

"Walter's got 'em."

"I figured that," I said. "So all you've got to do now is tell me where Walter and his buddies are."

Tony licked his lips and looked down at the two envelopes full of money.

"I get one of these envelopes if I tell?"

"That's right."

"Which one?"

I touched the one that had twenty-five thousand in it and moved it forward a bit.

"This one."

He wet his lower lip again, and I thought he was going to drool.

"I want 'em both."

"No."

"Then two."

"No."

"My brother says he can get half a million for the pictures he wants," he said, a crafty glint coming into his eye. "I figure I'm saving somebody that much money by tellin' you. That's gotta be worth seventy-five grand."

It wasn't my money, but for some reason I didn't want to give in.

I moved the one envelope back and pushed the other forward.

"Okay, that one."

Now he was thinking fifty grand *and* the girl. I felt sorry for him, because if he kept Caitlin with him she'd find a way to pry the money away from him.

"Come on, Tony," I said. "Where are they?"

"Walter's gettin' ready to send some of the pictures to the newspapers," he said. "He says he's tired of bein' jerked around."

"Well, it was you and Caitlin and her boyfriend who started jerkin' him around," I pointed out. "I'm sure he doesn't appreciate havin' to look for the three of you. If he finds you what do you think he'll do?"

"He'll kill me and Caitlin both."

"So if I give you this money, and make sure Walter goes to jail," I said, "you and Caitlin will be free and clear."

He thought that over.

"All you've got to do is tell me where to find him," I prodded.

Finally, I could see by the expression on his face and his body language that he'd come to a decision.

"I don't really . . . know where they are . . . exactly."

"What?"

"I don't know where he is, I swear," he said, quickly, "but I got a phone number."

If I gave the phone number to Joe Kennedy he could probably have it traced, but if Tony was right and his brother was getting ready to release the photo something had to be done right away.

"Okay," I said, "let's get you a phone."

Sixty-three

WE PUT CAITLIN BACK in with Tony and took the money out into the hall. When I picked the three envelopes up from the table Tony looked like he was going to cry.

Out in the hall we were joined by Larry Bigbee.

"What's up?" he asked. "Did you get what you want?"

"Not yet," I said. "Can we keep them in there a little longer?"

"Hey," Larry said, "be my guest. It's a slow night for cheaters and drunks."

He turned and walked off down the hall.

"What do we got?" Jerry asked.

"Caitlin was wrong. Tony doesn't know where his brother is. Apparently, they're not that close. But he does have a phone number."

"Will he call 'im?"

"He's the little brother," I said. "He's got a lot of resentment. Plus he wants the money and the girl all for himself."

"That dame'll eat him alive."

"I know," I said. "And she'd end up with the money."

"So what do we do? Pay 'im?"

"String him along," I said. "Get him to call his brother and either find out where he is or arrange a meet."

"Then what?"

"I'd make a phone call," I said, "but I have a feeling we need quicker action than that."

"You got action pretty quick last time."

"Somebody just had to go to the bank," I said. "This needs something more personal."

"I'm with you, Mr. G.," he said. "Whatever you wanna do."

"Ordinarily, I'd call the cops and hand this over to them."

"But the cops are lookin' for us."

"I know," I said. "Hargrove would be in too much of a hurry to bury us to listen to what we have to say."

"So it's you and me?"

"I guess so," I said, again aware of the weight of the gun in my pocket—the gun I had not yet had a reason to use.

"How do you want to play it?" Jerry asked.

"I'd like to set it up someplace familiar," I said, "but somehow I don't think Walter's as dumb as his brother, Tony."

He nodded.

"We'll have to give him something to say that his brother will buy."

"Like what?"

I started pacing the hall. "Gimme a minute or two . . ."

When we went back inside, I explained to Tony what I had come up with.

"If I do this I get the money?" he asked.

"Yes."

"And what do I get?" Caitlin asked. "This isn't fair, Eddie."

"Relax, baby," Tony said, putting his hand on her arm. "You get me."

I saw her arm jerk, as if her first instinct was to pull away, but she caught herself, leaned into him and smiled.

"You're my man, baby," she cooed to him.

Tony puffed out his sallow chest, looking inordinately proud of himself.

"Get me a phone," he said to me.

✳ ✳ ✳

Tony made the call while I listened on an extension. I asked him if his brother would hear in his voice that he was lying.

"Shit, man, I been lying for a living for years," he assured me.

The phone rang four times before a man answered. . . .

"*What?*"

"*Hey, bro.*"

"*Tony? What the fuck you want, man? Where are you? With that crazy bitch?*"

"*Hey,*" Tony said, "*don't talk about my lady like that.*"

Walter snorted into the phone.

"*Don't make me laugh, Tony. That bitch is bad news.*"

"*Yer just jealous.*"

"*Oh yeah, about you and that little girl? I'm busy, Tony. Why'd you call?*"

"*We made our buy.*"

"*What? You mean the Sammy Dav— You sonofabitch! I told you—*"

"*I know what you told me, but we got our price. Seventy-five grand.*"

"*Seventy-five! That's chickenfeed compared to what we're gonna get.*"

"*Yeah, well, you get nothin' without a buyer.*" *Tony looked at me, smiled slyly, and nodded.*

"*And you've got one?*"

"*Yah, big brother, I do. That go-between the nigger picked.*"

"*Listen, he's got your money. He wants to meet and he wants the pictures plus the negatives.*"

There was silence on the other end, and except for the fact that I didn't hear a click I thought he might have hung up.

"*Little brother, if you're fuckin' with me—*"

More silence.

"*Okay, set up a meet.*"

"*I want a piece.*"
I started toward him. Tony waved me away.
"*I want a piece, Walter. Yer gettin' a lot of money.*"
"*You'll get a piece, Tony,*" Walter said. "*I promise.*"
"*Okay,*" Tony said, "*write this down. . . .*"

Sixty-four

WHEN TONY HUNG UP I SAID, "You added to the script, trying to clip your brother for more money."

"He can afford it," he said. "Yer gonna give him a bundle."

I couldn't believe he actually thought I wanted to meet with Walter to pay him.

"Tell me, Tony, what will Walter do now?"

"Whataya mean?"

"When I show up with the money is he gonna give me the photos?"

"He'll have Denny and Paul with him."

"And they'll all be armed?"

"Oh yeah."

"So he'll try to kill me."

"Yup," Tony said. "He don't want nobody to be able to ID him."

"And that includes you and Caitlin, right?"

"Yeah," Tony said.

"It doesn't matter that you're his brother?"

"We're half brothers, and he don't care about that. He never did. He always treated me like shit. Well, now it's my turn."

I signaled Jerry to step outside with me.

"Hey," Tony said, as we went out the door. "What about my money?"

Before I closed the door I heard Caitlin say bitterly, "You asshole . . ."

We found Larry and I said, "Look, I need to hold them until I get back."

"Do I need to okay this with Mr. Entratter?" he asked.

"You can if you want to."

Bigbee took a deep breath and blew it out.

"Naw, okay, how long?"

"With any luck," I said, "there'll be some cops here in a few hours to pick them up."

"Cops would be a welcome sight," Larry said. "I'd like these two off my hands."

"This is on the up and up, Larry," I said. "I promise you."

"Okay, Eddie."

Larry walked over to the door and locked it.

"Okay," I said, turning to Jerry, "we've got about three hours to get ready."

"I think," he said, looking beyond me, "it might take us a little bit longer."

I turned and saw Detective Hargrove and several uniformed cops coming down the hall toward us.

"Larry—" I said.

Larry came back to us, shrugged and said, "Sorry, Eddie. I didn't have a choice. They came in lookin' for you and said we had to call if we saw you."

"So while we were questioning Caitlin and Tony you called them?"

"It's a question of keeping our license," he said.

"Or your job."

I reached for him but he backed away and bounced off of Jerry, who pushed him back toward me.

"Eddie—" Larry said, warningly.

"That's enough," Hargrove snapped. "Officers, cuff both of these men."

"Hargrove," I said, turning to face the detective, "you don't understand—"

"I understand that I finally caught you dirty, Gianelli," Hargrove said as his officers put the bracelets on me and Jerry. He moved close enough for me to smell what he had for lunch or dinner. "Haulin' you downtown is a pleasure I've been waitin' for since last year. You don't have your Rat Pack buddies to get you out, this time."

"Hargrove—"

He backed away from me and snapped, "Take 'em downtown!"

Sixty-five

THEY PUT US IN SEPARATE rooms. I had a nice big clock on the wall staring down at me so I could see that we were going to miss our meet. And if that happened there was going to be an embarrassing photo—or worse—of JFK in the papers the next morning.

Hargrove came in, closing the door gently behind him. The irony of the situation wasn't lost on me. Half an hour ago I was in his place, Tony and Caitlin were in mine.

"What happened to the two people we were holding?" I asked.

"You were holding?" he said. "You've got no right to hold anybody, Gianelli."

"What happened to them?"

"You got enough to worry about, Eddie," he said. "You and your buddy are in deep shit."

"We didn't do anything."

"I've got you for flight," he said, "at least."

"We didn't know you were lookin' for us."

"Like hell. I've also got a bullet in your wall that matches a gun that killed one of four dead men we found in an abandoned warehouse on Industrial Road."

"I haven't been home in a while."

"Staying away until your rug dries?" he asked. "What'd you do, shampoo out the bloodstains?"

"Did you have a warrant to go into my house?"

"You asked me that last time," Hargrove said, "and this time I did."

"Hargrove, you don't understand. You have to let me out of here. In two hours I have to—"

"You're gonna be here longer than that, Eddie," he said. "If you've got a date she's gonna get stood up."

"I've got a date all right," I said, "but it's not with a woman."

"Woman, guy, it doesn't matter," he said, "you're gonna miss it— but I didn't think you went that way."

"Goddammit, you don't understand," I said, "let me explain somethin' to you—"

"Why don't you start by tellin' me what happened in your house?" he asked. "And what you have to do with four dead guys?"

"I didn't—"

"And a set-up to make it look like they killed each other," he went on. "That sounds like somethin' your buddy Jerry brought with him from New York."

I was getting frustrated, but there was no way I could admit to any involvement with the dead men. That would put Jerry in the shitter, and I couldn't do that to him.

I sat forward and looked him in the eye.

"Hargrove," I said, "somethin' is gonna happen tonight that will impact—" I stopped short. Impact what? What could I tell him? The Presidency? I was supposed to be keeping that information to myself.

"Impact what?" he asked. "World peace?"

I was stuck for a reply.

"Sit tight," he said, moving toward the door. "I'm gonna go talk to your buddy. Maybe he'll give you up."

"Hargrove wait—" I said, but he was out the door, and he didn't return for almost an hour.

I knew Jerry wouldn't give me up, but time was ticking away. We had to get out of there and make that meet, but how? Hargrove was right. Frank, or Dean, or Sammy couldn't help me. It would take Jack Entratter a while to get a lawyer for us.

By the time Hargrove returned I had an idea.

"Am I under arrest?" I asked. "Are Jerry and I under arrest?"

"As a matter of fact," he said, "you are. Your only chance is to come clean—"

"I get a phone call," I said. "I want my phone call."

"A lawyer's not gonna help you—"

"I'm not talkin' to you until after my phone call," I told him.

He glared at me. If he wanted to he could keep me away from a phone long enough to ruin everything, but I was counting on him being the letter-of-the-law kind of guy he was.

"Hargrove, I'll talk to you," I said, "but after my phone call."

He frowned, then backed up and opened the door.

"Find me a room with a phone," he told the cop just outside the door.

Hargrove took me into a room with a phone. I stared at him until he got the message and headed for the door.

"I'll be right outside," he said. "You've three minutes."

As soon as the door closed I took a piece of paper out of my pocket and dialed the number on it.

A half hour later we were back in the other room and I was still trying to string Hargrove along. He was getting pissed.

"You haven't told me a thing, Eddie," he said. "You're doin' somethin' for another high roller that you can't talk about, and you don't know anythin' about bodies in a warehouse, or a bullet hole in your wall."

"That's it."

"You're wastin' my time," he said. "I think it's time we put you and your friend in a cell—separate cells—and let you sweat it out overnight."

I looked at the clock on the wall and he noticed.

"Yeah, you're gonna miss your date, pal," he said. "Let's have your wallet, belt and shoes." He'd already taken the envelopes of money.

If he put me in a cell that'd be the end of it. And if he went through my pockets thoroughly he'd find the photo, the one Sammy didn't want anyone to see. Would Hargrove recognize the person in it, I wondered?

I was fishing my wallet out when there was a knock on the door and a cop stuck his head in.

"Detective? You better come out here."

When he came back in he gave me an evil look.

"You think you're pretty smart, Eddie."

"Do I?"

"You really did it this time," he said. "You went straight to the top to cover your ass. I wonder who and what you're gonna have to pay for this?"

"I don't get you."

"You're out." He looked at my wallet and belt, which were on the table. He dug into his pocket, tossed the envelopes of money down reluctantly. "Put those away."

"Look, Detective," I said, "I didn't have a choice, here . . ."

I looked at the clock. We had fifty minutes.

"This must be some pretty hot date," he said. "You better enjoy it, because if I have anything to say about it, it'll be your last."

I put my wallet and the money away and slipped my belt back on. "Can I go?"

"Yeah," he said. "Your friend's waitin' outside."

I started past him, but he grabbed my arm in a grip like a vice.

"How high do your friends go, Eddie?"

I didn't answer.

"Pretty high, I think," he went on. "You know, when you get that high there's a heavy price to pay."

"I should be able to explain this to you later. . . ." I offered.

"Save it for your defense," he said. "You're gonna need it."

He let go of my arm and I went out the door.

Sixty-six

I FOUND JERRY OUTSIDE.

"Did you see anybody?" I asked. "Talk to anybody?"

"Nope," he said. "They just let me go. What happened?"

"I made a phone call."

"That number?" he asked.

"Yeah, that number," I said. "Come on, we gotta get a cab."

In the Sands parking lot minutes later, in my car, Jerry said, "We could call the cops and have them picked up."

"Hargrove would never go for it."

"There are other cops."

"Picked up for what?" I asked. "The most they'd get them for would be carrying guns."

"If we do this," he said, "you're gonna have to use that gun."

"Unless we can talk them out of it."

Jerry shook his head.

"These bozos are tryin' ta hold up the government," he said. "You ain't gonna talk them outta nothin'."

"You're probably right."

"You ever killed anybody with a gun before, Mr. G.?" he asked.

"In the army."

"Up close?"

"No."

"I got your back, Mr. G.," Jerry said. "I gotta know that you got mine."

I looked at him.

"You can ask me that after what happened in my house?"

"You didn't have ta shoot nobody," he said, "and you killed that guy by a fluke. Tonight ain't gonna be no fluke."

I took the gun out of my pocket and held it in my hand.

"Don't worry, big guy," I said, "I've got your back."

We pulled into the same parking lot behind the same warehouse. It was the only place we could think of that would be away from people. At first we thought about having them meet us on our ground, in a casino, but with them being armed there was a possibility that innocent people could be hurt.

We got out of the car and walked to the same door we'd used to enter the warehouse the other two times. There was yellow crime scene tape across the door, but it had been broken. Either someone had gone inside previously, or they were in there now.

We looked around the lot. There was no light other than the head-lights from my car.

"Let's cut the car lights, Jerry," I said. We both had flashlights this time.

He went to the car and turned off the lights. When he came back he had a flashlight in his left hand, and a gun in his right.

I took the gun out of my pocket, adopted the same position.

"Mr. G., you're gonna do the talkin', but you gotta let me have the lead on the action, okay?"

"Okay."

"It would've been better if we coulda arranged for some back-up," he said. "Gettin' picked up really fucked any chance for a plan."

"I know," I said. "I guess we should just go in and get it over with."

"We don't have ta do this, ya know," he said. "You don't have ta."

"First, I'm not lettin' you go in there alone," I said. "That's out. Second, yeah, I do have to do this, if just to get Hargrove off my back. Once he knows what was goin' on maybe I'll be off the hook for that bullet in my wall bein' connected to a murder weapon."

"Or not," he said.

"Yeah, well, let's be a little more optimistic here."

"Okay, Mr. G. You ready?"

I took a deep breath. Was I ready?

No.

"Yes."

Sixty-seven

WE STEPPED INSIDE and switched on our flashlights. It was quiet but then, in quick succession, other flashlights were turned on.

One . . . two . . . three . . .

. . . four and five.

"This ain't good," Jerry said in my ear. "There was only supposed to be three."

I nodded, then said, "Yes," because he probably couldn't see me nod.

"Walter?" I shouted.

The five points of light came closer to us, but stayed spread out. Jerry and I played our lights across them, saw five guys in their thirties who, like us, were holding lights and guns.

"You're outgunned," someone said. "Put 'em down."

"I don't think so," I said.

"We can put you down and take the money."

"If we have the money on us," I countered.

"You better have it on you."

"Look, if you start shootin' we'll start shootin'. You might kill us, but some of you won't leave this place alive. So why don't we just do business?"

That was met with silence.

"Walter? Is that you doin' the talkin'?"

More silence, then, "No, it's me." Then: "Jerry, is that you?"

The speaker shone his light on Jerry, who returned the favor. Jerry's light showed a black-haired guy in his thirties.

"Hey, Angelo," Jerry said. "What're you doin' with these amateurs?"

"Somebody killed the pros I was usin'," he pointed at me, "left them all in here. I didn't have any idea who killed them . . . up ta now . . ."

"That's too bad," Jerry said.

"What're you doin' with him?"

"Mr. G., this here's Angelo DeLucca," Jerry said. "Angelo, meet Eddie Gianelli. He's a good friend of Mr. Sinatra's."

"So what?" Angelo said, looking unimpressed.

"Does Handsome Johnny know what you're up to, Angelo?" Jerry asked.

I knew "Handsome Johnny" was Johnny Roselli, who represented Sam Giancana in Vegas, as well as Hollywood. In fact, some folks said Roselli was employed by Monogram Studios as a producer.

I did the math in my head: DeLucca/Roselli, Roselli/Giancana, Giancana/Sinatra, Sinatra/Sammy Davis, not to mention Sinatra/JFK and it wasn't hard to figure out how this Angelo might know about Sammy's photos. It wouldn't take much for DeLucca to have someone creep into Sammy's house for the film.

"Just tryin' to do some business on the side, Jerry," Angelo said. "You know how that is."

"I do know, Angelo," Jerry said, "but I'd never cross Mr. Giancana this way."

"I ain't crossin' MoMo," Angelo said. "This dough ain't comin' outta his pocket."

"Yeah, you tell him that," Jerry said. "You tell him how you used his connection to Mr. Sinatra to not only hold up Sammy Davis Jr., but President Kennedy."

"Hey, that wasn't me tryin' ta squeeze the nigger," Angelo said. "That was Ernie and his girl, and Walter's idiot brother."

"Where's Tony?" a voice asked. I assumed it was Walter.

"I'm not sure, Walter," I said. "Up to half an hour ago the cops had him."

"The cops?"

"I told you," DeLucca said, wearily, "I told you to keep that idiot away from us."

"I didn't—"

DeLucca turned and fired one shot. One of the flashlights fell to the floor. That was the end of Walter.

"Easy," DeLucca said, as we all jumped at the sound of his shot. "Just doin' some housecleanin'."

And cutting the odds for us, I thought. Two to one, now.

"Too bad," DeLucca said, looking back at Jerry and me. "He was a waiter at the Sands last year when JFK came to see the Rat Pack."

"Ah," I said, "so he spotted Sammy takin' a picture, saw somethin' in the background that would be worth money, if it was played right."

"He was always hangin' around me," DeLucca said, "wantin' a job. When he came to me with this I knew how to play it."

"Right," I said, "sit on it until JFK got comfortable in the Presidency."

"Right," DeLucca said, "but he was actually as big an idiot as his brother. He kept that six-gun he took when he creeped the nigger Jew's house."

"He did the house?" Jerry asked.

"He went with one of my men," Angelo said. "Spotted the guns, decided to take one."

"So why did you leave it on the body?" I asked.

"Why not? I knew Walter had it on him, so after I killed Ernie I took it from him and left it there. Give the cops somethin' ta think about."

"But why frame—"

"Where's the fuckin' money?" DeLucca demanded, cutting me off.

I wondered if we could cut the odds down a little more.

"You guys see that?" I asked. "That's what he's got in mind for all of you."

"Shut up," Angelo DeLucca said. "Shut yer friend up, Jerry."

"Why, Angelo?" Jerry asked. "He's right, ain't he? You ain't gonna share any of the money with these bozos. I'll bet they was all brought into the game by Walter, right? And now you shot their friend down right in front of them."

"A four-way split is better than five," DeLucca announced to his cohorts.

"And a one way split is the best of all," I said. "Come on, guys, Angelo here is a pro. He knows how to tie up loose ends, and you guys are all loose ends."

"You're the biggest loose end," Angelo said to me. "I should take care of you right now."

He extended his gun toward me.

"Don't Ang—" Jerry said, but he had no time to finish. He had no choice but to fire. The shot lit up the room. The bullet hit Angelo dead center. He spasmed, pulled the trigger of his own gun, firing a round wild and lighting the darkness again.

That left three of them and two of us.

"Drop 'em, boys," Jerry said. "It's all over."

We played our lights over them. They were all nervous, jittery, sweating and biting their lips, wondering what to do because the two men who were their leaders were gone. If they panicked and started shooting it wasn't going to go well.

Suddenly, we heard what sounded like a bolt being thrown and the sliding metal door to the bay slid up. The glare of several sets of headlights lit the interior of the warehouse and nearly a dozen men came charging in with guns.

"Drop 'em, everybody!" somebody yelled. "Federal agents."

One guy got antsy and turned his gun toward them. He caught three slugs and went down. In quick succession his buddies met the same fate, and then it was just me and Jerry standing.

"Take it easy!" I yelled, and we put our hands in the air.

I had no doubt these were Joe Kennedy's men. He'd sprung us after my phone call, and then obviously had us followed. Now the question was, what were their orders where we were concerned?

"You Eddie Gianelli?" one of the agents asked.

If I said yes would they gun us down? Tie up the last of the loose ends?

I had to play the hand that had been dealt to me.

"I'm Gianelli."

The dead men were being searched by other agents, and one of them came up with a brown manila envelope. He brought it over to the man who'd questioned me, obviously the agent in charge. The envelope had blood on it, but that didn't seem to bother him. He had a flashlight of his own. He opened the envelope, shined the light in, and then closed it. All he'd been able to see was that there were photos and negatives inside, but I didn't think he'd been able to see what they were photos of.

He folded the envelope lengthwise, stuck it in his inside jacket pocket, then turned his attention back to his men.

"Pack it in!" he yelled.

The agents brought in plastic bags, which they used to remove the bodies. I still wasn't sure what they were going to do with us.

The agent-in-charge looked at us as his men cleaned up the scene and said, "Mr. Kennedy's compliments. You and your buddy better get out of here."

Jerry and I looked at each other. If they hadn't shot us by now they weren't going to shoot us as we left.

"You don't have to tell us twice," I said, and we got the hell out of there.

Sixty-eight

As soon as Sammy opened his door I handed him the photo and the negative.

"Come on in."

I entered, closing the door behind me. It was the morning after and Jerry had remained in Vegas. I wanted to get the photo back to Sammy right away.

"Did you . . . look at it?"

"Once," I said, "just to make sure it was the right one."

"We were just . . . bein' silly," he said, looking embarrassed, "and I had one shot left. May . . . isn't usually this . . . free with her body—"

"You don't have to explain anything to me."

"Not that she's a prude," he went on, "but, man, if this picture had gotten into the papers—you dig?"

"Yeah," I said, "I do."

He put his hand out and I shook it, then he pulled me into a big hug.

"Thanks, Eddie. Man, I owe you."

"You're welcome."

He put the photo and negative into his pocket, then asked, "And the other thing? You fix that, too?"

"I hope so," I said.

I didn't want to tell him there could have been more prints out there, that there was still the possibility that a photo of a naked May Britt, or a compromised JFK, could still show up in the newspapers or a magazine. It seemed like all the guilty parties were either dead or— as in the case of Caitlin and Tony—in jail, at the moment.

Apparently, the same phone call that had sprung me and Jerry had sealed Caitlin and Tony's fate. When I had gone to sleep the night before I was almost expecting to be awakened by cops at my door, but the morning dawned with no such intrusion. Hargrove may have still had it in for me, but for the moment I seemed to be in the clear.

"Did you hear about Joe Kennedy?" Sammy asked.

"What about him?"

"He had a stroke," Sammy said. "Yesterday."

"Dead?" I asked.

"No, but pretty bad. They think he'll be in a wheelchair from now on."

"That's too bad," I said. "Guess I was one of the last to see him on his feet. He was . . . pretty damn impressive."

"Who did it, Eddie?" he asked. "Who broke into my house and stole the photos?"

I told him.

I spent the night in the room at the Sands, and that's where Jerry still was, but it was time for me to go home. I needed to talk to Jack Entratter, but I was putting that off for later in the day.

The rug had dried, the bullet hole was still in the door frame, but the bullet was gone. Hargrove had it.

Could he use it to come after me again? Now that Joe Kennedy was incapacitated? Well, it wasn't as if I hadn't been looking over my shoulder for him ever since the first time we met. So nothing had really changed.

I was making a pot of coffee when the phone rang. What I needed to do was sit quietly, drain the pot by myself, and finally stop shaking from the confrontation in the warehouse.

"Hello?"

"Eddie?"

"That's right."

"It's Jack."

I didn't say anything.

"Jack Kennedy. The President?" he added.

"I know who you are."

"I'm sorry to call so unexpectedly," JFK said, "but I wanted to thank you for what you did."

"I, uh, was under the impression that you didn't know what was going on."

"Oh I didn't," he said, "until my father had his stroke. Then I was told."

Yeah, right.

"So . . . it was you who got me sprung last night?"

"Yes."

Hargrove didn't know how right he'd been about my connections going higher.

"Of course, no one knows it was me, and I'd like to keep it that way."

"Of course."

"You did your country a great service, Eddie."

"Um, well, okay." Now was not the time to tell him I was glad I didn't vote for him.

There was a moment of silence, and then he asked, "Uh, you didn't see the photo, did you, Eddie?"

"What photo was that, Mr. President?"

Epilogue

THE SHOW ACTUALLY BROUGHT tears to my eyes. Sandy Hackett and his troupe of players had the guys down pat. Sandy himself did a great job playing Joey. Even hearing Buddy Hackett's voice do the opening made me mist up. I had last seen Buddy in 2003, just before he passed away, and I missed him.

And the fella playing Sammy was perfect. He made me miss Sammy so much I looked down at the gold watch I was wearing, the one Sammy had given me for helping him out in 1961.

I should have gone backstage to congratulate them but I didn't. I couldn't. Didn't want to make an old fool of myself.

I fell in with the flow of people filing out and, once outside, buttoned my coat. The chill in the desert was getting to my old bones more than usual.

I stood to the side, allowing the rest of the crowd to file past me. At my age being jostled could amount to the same as being shoved off a cliff.

Finally, the crowd was gone and I stood outside the Greek Isles virtually alone—until I heard someone call my name from behind. I turned to see Sandy approaching me, still in his Joey makeup.

"You runnin' out on me?" he asked.

"To tell you the truth," I said, "your show got to me. Brought back a lot of memories. I—I wasn't sure I could . . ."

"I know what you mean," he said. "My dad's only been gone four years but every time I hear his voice . . ."

We stood there together, a moment of silence for the departed, the friends and loved ones from our past. . . .

Oh yeah, next time you watch *Sergeants 3* check me out. I got last billing as "Man with snake."

Author's Note

As I've said before, these books grew out of my respect for Dean Martin, Frank Sinatra and Sammy Davis Jr. as entertainers—not necessarily in that order. My posthumous thanks goes out to these three men for years of enjoyment through their films, albums and many appearances on stage. Also, my thanks to Joey Bishop, the last of the Rat Pack, who died this past year.

The books also stem from my love for the history, the pulse, the excitement that is Las Vegas. There's no other place in the world like it.

Special thanks to Kathy War, Photo Archivist, UNLV Libraries, Special Collections Department for the time and effort she put into talking with me and providing me with archive photos of the Sands Casino. And to Sandy Hackett, for allowing me to use him and his Rat Pack tribute show in this book. And finally, thanks to Richard Neuberger, Jack Entratter's nephew, for contacting me after reading the first book. Thanks for the kind words, and for talking with me on the phone about your Uncle Jack.

Bibliography

Rat Pack Confidential by Shawn Levy, Doubleday, 1998; *The Rat Pack* by Lawrence J. Quirk and William Schoell, 1998; *Dino* by Nick Tosches, Dell Publishing, 1992; *His Way, The Unauthorized Biography of Frank Sinatra* by Kitty Kelley, Bantam Books, 1986; *Gonna Do Great Things, The Life of Sammy Davis, Jr.* by Gary Fishgall, Scribners, 2003; *Sammy Davis Jr., Me and My Shadow* by Arthur Silber Jr., Smart Enterprises, 2002; *Sammy: An Autobiography* by Sammy Davis Jr. and June and Burt Boyar, Farrar, Straus and Giroux, 2000; *Photo by Sammy Davis, Jr.,* text by Burt Boyar, Regan Books, 2007; *The Peter Lawford Story, Life with the Kennedys, Monroe and the Rat Pack* by Patricia Seaton Lawford, Carroll & Graf Publishers, 1988; *Mouse in the Rat Pack, The Joey Bishop Story* by Michael Seth Starr, Taylor Trade Publishing, 2002; *The Frank Sinatra Film Guide* by Daniel O'Brien, BT Batsford, 1998; *The Last Good Time, Skinny D'Amato, The Notorious 500 Club, and The Rise and Fall of Atlantic City* by Jonathan Van Meter, Crown Publishers, 2003; *Casino, Love and Honor in Las Vegas* by Nicholas Pileggi, Simon & Schuster, 1995; *Las Vegas is My Beat* by Ralph Pearl, Bantam Books, 1973, 1974; *Murder in Sin City, The Death of a Las Vegas Casino Boss* by Jeff German, Avon Books, 2001; *A Short History of Reno,* by Barbara and Myrick

Land, University of Nevada Press, 1995; *A Short History of Las Vegas* by Barbara and Myrick Land, University of Nevada Press, 1999, 2004; and *When the Mob Ran Vegas* by Steve Fischer, Berkline Press, 2005, 2006.